RUTH

One of the Bible's enduring stories of love, courage, and faith

"Go with my blessing," Naomi said.

Orpah seemed to hang irresolutely between Naomi and the door, and then she clutched her robe around her and ran into the morning.

Naomi watched her go, and Ruth could not tell what she was feeling, so expressionless was her face. Slowly Naomi turned to Ruth.

"See," she said, "see what she has done. She has gone, and wisely, I suspect, back to her people and her gods. Won't you do the same? Won't you, my dear?"

What can I say that will make it clear to her that it won't matter if I'm lonely or homesick or if I have regrets about leaving ⋯⋯⋯⋯⋯⋯⋯⋯⋯⋯⋯⋯ to her husba⋯

"M⋯⋯⋯⋯⋯⋯⋯⋯⋯⋯⋯⋯⋯⋯ to talk and h⋯⋯⋯⋯⋯⋯⋯⋯⋯⋯⋯⋯⋯ d that her ⋯⋯⋯⋯⋯⋯⋯⋯⋯⋯⋯⋯⋯⋯ hing Ruth⋯⋯⋯⋯⋯⋯⋯⋯⋯⋯⋯⋯⋯ un- ders⋯⋯⋯⋯⋯⋯⋯⋯⋯⋯⋯⋯⋯, I'll stay.⋯

N⋯

"F⋯⋯⋯⋯⋯⋯⋯⋯⋯⋯⋯⋯⋯⋯ ople and ⋯

Lois T. Henderson

By the same author

Hagar
Abigail
Lydia
Miriam

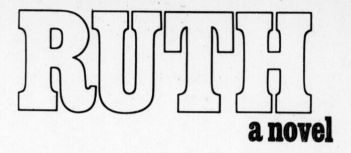

RUTH
a novel

Lois T. Henderson

1817

Harper & Row, Publishers, San Francisco

New York, Grand Rapids, Philadelphia, St. Louis
London, Singapore, Sydney, Tokyo, Toronto

Ruth was published in a hardcover edition by Christian Herald Books. Reprinted by agreement.

FIRST HARPER & ROW PAPERBACK EDITION

Library of Congress Cataloging in Publication Data

Henderson, Lois T.
  RUTH.

  1. Ruth (Biblical character)—Fiction.   I. Title.
PS3558.E486R8   1981b   813'.54   82-48400
ISBN 0-06-063864-8

90 91 92 93 94 95 MPC 20 19 18 17 16 15 14 13 12

In loving memory of
my father-in-law and mother-in-law,
The Rev. Samuel C. and Laura W. Henderson,
and of my dear friend
Ruth M. Curry

Acknowledgments

I would like to express my gratitude to several people whose assistance lightened my task of writing this book. I am grateful to Gladys Donaldson for her criticism and suggestions and to my editor, William Chickering, for his encouragement and help. Without the aid of Margaret Wilson, town and church librarian, and Dikran Hadidian, librarian of Barbour Library at Pittsburgh Theological Seminary, my research would have been much more difficult than it was. I want to express thanks to my nephew, Robert Richardson, who spent part of his vacation helping with the typing of the manuscript.

Finally, I am grateful to my mother-in-law, Laura W. Henderson, who taught me the privilege of being a daughter-in-law, and to my daughter-in-law, Mary Ann Henderson, who daily teaches me the joys of being a mother-in-law.

part I

Now they entered the land of Moab and remained there. Then Elimelech, Naomi's husband, died; and she was left with her two sons. And they took...Moabite women as wives...Orpah and...Ruth.... Then both Mahlon and Chilion also died; and the woman was bereft.

Ruth 1: 2*b*-4*a*, 5*a*

1

THE EARLY MORNING SKY, rinsed clean by the recent winter rains, curved overhead as though it were an inverted bowl. Ruth, striding toward the well, paused for a moment and tipped back her head to look at it.

If we could find a clay that would turn blue when it was fired, she mused, how beautiful the pots would be. Or even a blue slip to trace on the outer surface of the bowls. Wouldn't it be lovely?

A familiar voice pulled her attention away from the sky.

"What are you looking for — birds to trap for dinner?"

Ruth grinned. The woman coming toward her was her sister but as unlike Ruth as it's possible for sisters to be. Small and oddly fair for a Moabite, Patima bore no resemblance to her tall, dark sister. Nor did her pointed, elfin face have any similarity to Ruth's calm, serene face with its broad forehead, winged brows and wide, mobile mouth.

"I was admiring the morning sky," Ruth said. "Don't you ever think of anything besides food to cook?"

Patima lengthened her steps to match Ruth's. "And you," she replied. "Don't you ever think of anything practical?"

"I was being practical," Ruth argued. "I was thinking how beautiful it would be if my husband could make pottery the color of that sky. Look at it! Summer sky is never like that. Only winter mornings have that clear, lovely color."

Patima didn't even glance up. "Your lord Mahlon would laugh at your fancy. How is he, by the way? And the pottery business? How does it go these days since his brother died? Can Mahlon manage alone?"

Ruth's face sobered. "We're doing well enough. I do as much of Chilion's work as I can; he was never very strong, you know. My husband seems to think we'll get along."

Patima looked down at Ruth's feet, so that Ruth was made uncomfortably aware of how stained and discolored they were.

"Don't you find the work hard?" Patima asked. "Tramping in the clay, for instance. Do your sister-in-law and mother-in-law help?"

"Of course they help. Orpah's really very clever, and she does a lot. When Chilion first died, of course, she was too grieved to even think of work. With no children to comfort her —" Ruth's voice trailed off.

"Yes, poor soul." Patima's voice was compassionate. "And it wasn't that she had any trouble conceiving. How many children has she lost? Three? Four?"

"Three," Ruth said. "None of them strong enough to live. In some ways, their deaths were even harder on my mother-in-law than on Orpah. She — Naomi, that is — says she's been cursed."

"I can understand that. Her husband dead — how long? ten years? — her older son dead six months now, and not a single grandchild to comfort her old age."

Ruth made a sudden move as though she were wincing with pain, and Patima hurried on. "Not that a woman can be blamed if she's childless. I know you try. I know that years ago you made sacrifice to our god, Chemosh. And to Ashtar, too. It's true that you've never joined the fertility rites, but —"

Ruth interrupted. "Naomi thinks the fertility rites are wicked. My lord Mahlon agrees with her. You know they insist that we speak only of Yahweh in our house."

Patima's glance held a mixture of pity and mischief. "Your mother-in-law is as much an Israelite as she was the day she left Bethlehem. She's a foreigner still, in spite of all her years in Moab. So she doesn't understand that Chemosh gives his people the fertility rites as part of our worship. The best part, in fact."

A clear wash of red ran up into Ruth's face. "You shock me," she snapped. "To talk like that on the street."

Patima laughed. "You won't ever change, will you? Don't you and your lord ever laugh together?"

Ruth was silent for a long time. The two women had nearly reached the well when she spoke. "We used to, but my lord Mahlon doesn't have much to laugh about anymore. He's responsible for three women, two of them widows. He has no children, no, nor the hope of one. And he's miles away from all who are kin to him. For all his success as a potter, we're not at all rich. What is there to laugh about?"

Patima tucked her hand into Ruth's arm with a rare gesture of affection. "I know," she said in a soothing tone. "I do understand your sorrow at being barren, and that it's not easy to be married to a foreigner." Patima hesitated and then went on in a suddenly bitter tone. "There's some good in being barren. At least you've never borne a child only to have him torn out of your arms to die."

Ruth stared at her sister in astonishment. The bitter words were totally unexpected. Patima was so merry, so serene most of the time that Ruth had almost come to believe that her sister had forgotten the birth and the death of her firstborn son.

But I have never forgotten, Ruth thought with anger. Even though he was not my child, even though I was unmarried at the time, even though....

She and Patima walked on in silence, but Ruth's mind had gone back more than ten years, back to the day when the terrifying threat of destruction had been brought by nomadic shepherds to Faran, the young and untried husband of Patima. His father had recently died, and Faran had just been named as head man of the village.

When the frightening news came to Faran, he had been

sitting over his supper, served by Patima while Ruth, who had come to help with the care of Patima's baby, sat quietly in a corner.

"There's a tribe of Edomites," the nomad said, almost babbling in his fear. "They've come over the border and claim they've been told by their god to destroy the town of Bezer. This town."

Faran stared at the messenger, his mouth full of food. "Why?" he finally said.

The nomad shrugged. "What difference does it make? They need rain or some other kind of blessing, and they think a village of dead Moabites will appease their god."

Faran looked at Patima and Ruth. "Call the elders of the village," he commanded. "Hurry. Tell them to come at once."

Ruth and Patima both ran, knocking on doors, calling out their alarming news. Then, followed by the elders, they hurried back to Faran's house.

The elders, all of them past the age of being able to work or fight, and their young leader recognized the danger of a raid from the north. Most of the young men of the village were out in the wilderness with the flocks; there would not be time to get them home and armed before the Edomites swept down on the village.

In the middle of the breathless discussion, Patima's baby began to cry, his shrill demand for food rising stridently over the babble of men's voices.

Patima hurried to pick him up and silence his noise against her breast, but the old priest of Chemosh rose from his place and came toward Patima, his rheumy eyes filled with speculation.

"This is your child?" he asked Faran.

"Yes. My first born. A boy." Faran's voice was warm with sudden pride.

The priest plucked the cover away from the small round head with its dark hair. "Perfect?" he asked.

Ruth wanted to cry out that the child was deformed, ill, ugly, but Faran, apparently ignorant of the priest's intentions, spoke with satisfaction. "Yes. Perfect. But why do you concern yourself with my son, my lord? We have graver matters to discuss."

The priest was silent, but Ruth saw comprehension dawning slowly on Faran's face. Horror followed the comprehension. Then, incredibly, the horror was replaced by submission. Terrified, Ruth tore her eyes away from her brother-in-law's face and looked at Patima. Was there no one to speak for this child?

"Our god, Chemosh," the priest cried out in a terrible voice, "will save us if we offer the smoke from burning flesh up to him. This child is the first born of Faran, the head of our village. As an offering to Chemosh, he could save us all from disaster."

Patima's voice was pulled out of her in a thin, high note of grief. "Oh, no. Not my baby. Oh, please —"

The priest stared at her with unblinking eyes, and Ruth watched the way Patima shriveled into silence. Moving like a sleep walker, Faran approached his wife and lifted the baby out of her arms. Deprived of food, the child began to wail. Faran did not even look down into the small, angry face. He carried the child to the priest and laid him on the skinny, outstretched arms.

"Quick, my lord," Faran begged. "The Edomites are even now coming toward our town."

"Oh, please," Ruth begged quietly to Patima, "don't let them do this. Don't let them —"

Faran, hearing her frantic whisper, turned abruptly toward the women. "Quiet!" he hissed. "Both of you. The priest of our god has spoken and we must obey."

"Don't you even care?" Ruth gasped.

"Do you want to be killed?" Faran grated, "You and everyone else in the village, and that includes *every* child. What is the death of one child compared to so many? Your sister can bear other children."

Patima's face was gray, but she was silent. The baby's cries were the only sound in the room.

The priest turned, carrying the baby before him as one

would carry a lamb to a sacrificial altar. One by one, the shuffling old men of Bezer, headed by Faran, followed him toward the small building that served as a temple.

For several moments, the two girls stood in silence, then Patima slowly sank to the floor, her face buried in her shaking hands.

"Why didn't you fight for him?" Ruth whispered.

"What do you know about it?" Patima responded dully. "You're not even fifteen years old yet. You don't know what it is to be married, to have to obey your husband —" Her voice trailed off as shuddering sobs shook her body.

Filled with pity, Ruth knelt beside her. Patima was only a year older, but she had always seemed wiser, more practical. Still — to give up one's child without a struggle —

"They had no right," Ruth said, even while her hand patted the prostrate girl beside her.

"Men have every right," Patima whimpered.

Sudden fury blazed through Ruth. "No," she cried. "There's such a thing as mercy, as pity —"

The words were cut off by the sudden shrill sound of chanting. Ruth froze with horror. Then, clearly, she heard the sound of the baby's angry, hungry cry.

Ruth flashed to her feet and raced out of the house. She wouldn't let it happen. No matter what anyone said, no merciful god would demand a baby's death. The amount of smoke from such a tiny body could mean nothing — nothing.

Her flying feet brought her to the door of the temple. The fire on the altar, which was always kept burning, had been fanned to a fierce heat. The elders stood on either side of the altar, forming an aisle, down which the chanting priest moved slowly, bearing the crying child toward the blaze.

Knowing she should not be there, knowing that no woman should be watching this ancient rite, still Ruth stood, unable to move, her fists pressed against her mouth.

Oh, please, she begged in silent agony and knew it was not to Chemosh that she prayed. Oh, please, not like that, alive and crying and *knowing*. Oh, please, please —

She wrapped her arms across her breast as though the child had been born of her own body, and the intensity of her pleading ran through her like the flames from the altar.

The priest faltered, peered down into the crying face of the child. His arms moved with a sort of spasm as though he would toss the living child into the flames. Then he hesitated.

The scene blurred before Ruth, but she was able to see that the child was placed almost gently on the stone before the altar. The priest's hands moved sharply, covering the baby's face, pressing down. The crying stopped.

Still hugging her arms across her chest, Ruth turned and fled, so she did not see the small body consumed by the hungry flames. She did not hear the chanting voices, the prayers of supplication. She did not even know that word came that the nomad had been misinformed. The Edomites had never planned to come to Bezer.

She ran until her legs gave out, until she crumpled, weeping, to the ground. It was all wrong, she thought. The baby should be alive, cuddled safely in Patima's arms. No one — no one had the right to do what the priest had done.

She didn't know how long she had lain there when a woman's voice roused her.

"Are you ill, my child?"

Ruth recognized the accent in the voice. The speaker must be Naomi, the foreigner who had come from Israel. They had met occasionally at the well.

Ruth raised her head, feeling swollen and sodden from her weeping. "They sacrificed the baby," she said woodenly.

Naomi's voice sharpened. "Who? What baby? You don't have a child."

"It was my sister's child. The elders heard we would be attacked by Edomites. They burned the child to please the god, Chemosh."

There was a pinched look on Naomi's face. "Our God, Yahweh, the Lord of the ends of the earth, does not demand such evil sacrifice."

Ruth nodded, grateful for the unexpected understanding. "No god who is good would kill a baby." Her voice broke. "He had only learned to smile."

Naomi sat on the ground beside her. "I'm sorry," she said simply.

Ruth buried her face in her hands again, but there was less anguish in her tears. At least, she thought, the priest didn't throw him alive into the flames. And there is a god, somewhere, who does not demand the death of babies to earn his mercy.

Naomi sat in silence, and when she finally spoke, her words were entirely unexpected. "Are you spoken for, my child? Has your father promised you in marriage?"

"No." Ruth spoke in muffled tones. "Not yet, although he's beginning to talk about it."

"Well, then," Naomi said and let her voice trail away. When she spoke again, she said only, "You must start home. It's close to sunset, and your sister will need you."

"Yes," Ruth agreed. "Thank you."

But Patima would not talk about what had happened, and Ruth was never able to offer any comfort. By the time Patima was pregnant again, Ruth was betrothed to Mahlon, son of Naomi, and there were other things to talk about.

Patima's voice, normal again with all the bitterness hidden away, brought Ruth back to the present. "Look," she said, "we got to the well for once before the whole village arrived. Even our mother is late."

"Then let's draw the water right away," Ruth said, feeling a little dazed from the remembering. "I have to hurry back anyhow. There's a batch of pots in the kiln which will have to be taken out by midday. I've no time to stay and gossip."

"Then you'd better draw your water first. If our mother comes while you're still here, you'll be held up for hours while she complains about her aches and pains."

Ruth shook her head. "She may complain, but she'd do anything for us, and you know it."

Patima's quick grin brightened her face. "You'd find something good to say about the forces of evil, I think. I wish some of your goodness had rubbed off on me."

Ruth only smiled but she felt the familiar stab of guilt. Everyone spoke of her goodness; no one seemed to even guess that anger and resentment were often bubbling under the surface. In one way, she was grateful that people thought well of her; in another way she longed for a deeper understanding than she had ever known.

Carefully, she lifted her dripping water jar. The smooth tan clay shone wet in the morning light, and the jar rested comfortably in the curve of Ruth's shoulder. Every woman in the town of Bezer wanted one of the Israelite potter's jars for the carrying of water. They had balance and grace and yet were lighter than most jars.

"I need a new jar," Patima said. "Our extra one was knocked from the shelf yesterday and broken into a hundred pieces. I'll be over sometime soon. And we'll pay the regular price," she added as though to forestall an old argument.

"You're my sister," Ruth began, but Patima interrupted.

"Don't be silly. My husband can afford a new water jar. You'd better hurry. I think I see our mother coming from her house."

"I'll see you tomorrow then," Ruth said quickly and turned to hurry down the narrow street that led to her own house.

2

RUTH WALKED along the narrow street, slowed down by the weight of her jar of water. Once, where there were no houses to block the view, she stopped to gaze around her. Piles of creamy clouds crowded across the sky, but the sun was strong and warm. After several days of pelting winter rain, the warmth felt good, and Ruth hunched her shoulders under her shawl, careful not to disturb the jar.

From where she stood, she could look across the small village to the fields in the valley that were beginning to show green with the planted crops, and then on to the tawny hills that made a low ridge between the Moab plateau and the Dead Sea.

She stood staring for a few minutes, aware of the vividness of the scene that was so often obscured by mist or shimmering heat waves or just the haze of familiarity. Then the realization that she had work to do, that she couldn't stand dreaming as though she had wealth and leisure time, made her turn and hurry toward the pottery that stood on the edge of town.

The pottery itself was a small building at the back of a hard packed yard which had a rounded earthen kiln in the center. On either side of the pottery were two small stone houses, built exactly alike of the honey colored stone of the region.

Ruth remembered the day that Mahlon had confided the reason his father had built two houses instead of one. Elimilech had not wanted the residents of Bezer to look on the newly arrived Israelites as beggars even though it was true that the famine in Bethlehem had taken their customers as well as their food supply. He had been determined that his sons would not come to marriage empty handed. Mahlon had confessed that he had always believed that the work and sacrifice needed to build the two houses had cost his father his life, but at least Elimelech had earned some respect in Bezer, enough respect that his widow had been able, after his death, to find Moabite wives for his sons.

She and Mahlon had been married several years, Ruth remembered, before he had trusted her enough to risk such a confidence. Even in marriage, foreigners were suspect. It was the way things were.

She carried her jar of water to the nearer of the two houses and set it on a shelf. Wiping her hands down the sides of her coarse skirt, she hurried across the yard toward the pottery. She stopped at the kiln long enough to add fuel to the banked fire and then entered the low door of the work room. She hesitated as the dimness spread before her sunstruck eyes.

"You're back so soon? Was there no one to gossip with, then?"

Mahlon's voice was mild, almost disinterested. Ruth turned to look at her husband. His shoulders were as stooped as an old man's from long hours at the potter's wheel, but his movements were vigorous. The circular wooden treadle moved under his feet, turning the stone wheel that held the clay. As she watched, her husband's slender fingers piled the clay coils on top of each other. She never failed to be amazed at the small miracle of the wet brown coils turning into a pot or jar.

"No one to gossip with?" he repeated, glancing up with a smile.

"There was my sister, my lord," she said, returning his smile. "She said they're going to need another water pot. The batch in the kiln has some particularly nice ones. And they'll be ready in just a few hours. Maybe she can get one of those."

"We'll never get rich having relatives as customers," Mahlon said.

"My lord," she began, but he interrupted.

"I'm not complaining. Wasn't it only yesterday that Orpah came for a cooking pot? It's all right."

"But Orpah is *your* relative, my lord, and it's our responsibility to see that she and your mother have what they need. My sister says she'll pay for anything she gets."

Mahlon's face was tight with frustration. "I don't need charity from the residents of this town."

"I'm the only sister Patima has," Ruth reminded him. "Is kindness from my family charity, my lord?"

Mahlon did not speak for the time it took him to smooth away the ridge left by the last loop of clay. Finally he lifted his head and looked at Ruth.

"Families can be both a joy and a responsibility," he said. He hesitated before adding, "Have you talked to my mother lately?"

"I talk to your mother every day, my lord."

"I mean, about anything special?"

"No, my lord, nothing special. Does she want something? Is she troubled?"

"Of course she's troubled. What do you expect of a woman who is a widow and whose son has only recently died?"

"I'm sorry, my lord. I didn't mean that. I know how she feels, or at least I can imagine. I just meant, is there anything I can do for her now?"

Mahlon's eyes dropped. "Never mind. She'll come to you when she's ready. She may not be ready yet."

"Ready for what, my lord?"

"Never mind," he repeated. "As soon as I've finished turning this pot, I want to wedge some clay. Get it out for me."

She turned to the bin where clay was kept damp under cloths of woven goat hair. Even though the clay had already been tramped and squeezed in the trough in the yard, it still had to be kneaded or wedged before it could be rolled into the clay ropes that Mahlon used. Ruth plunged her hands into the wet stuff and pulled out a mass of it.

"Let me wedge it, my lord," she suggested. She looked from her own broad, capable hands to Mahlon's artistic, slender ones. "You have to work so hard now that you're alone. Let me knead the clay."

"I'm sure you're thinking only of me," Mahlon said, his voice tired and a little sarcastic. "You're not thinking at all of the two pots that exploded last week in the kiln because all the moisture had not been kneaded out."

"It may not have been your fault, my lord. Perhaps I tried to fire them too soon."

"Maybe," Mahlon said. "Oh, well, go ahead. You can at least start the wedging."

If only I had given him sons, Ruth thought, as she started the rhythmic kneading, I wouldn't feel so guilty all the time. I'd feel I had done something of value. As it is, I've done nothing. That I can knead the clay is small comfort.

They worked in silence until Orpah suddenly appeared at the door of the workroom.

"I've been spinning all morning," she said. "But now my husband's mother said I should come and take the pots out of the kiln. Do you think they're ready?"

Ruth looked up, glad to stop and rest her aching shoulders. She saw with some surprise that Mahlon hardly glanced at Orpah. He had made an effort to be kind to her since the death of his brother, but today he seemed uneasy, almost as though he were embarrassed.

"Good morning, Orpah," Ruth cried, covering up Mahlon's silence. "How are you and our mother this morning?"

Orpah smiled. Her white widow's clothes made her skin dark and warm, and her eyes, heavy from her many days of weeping, were large and shadowed. Because Orpah was tiny and delicate, Ruth always felt a little awkward beside her.

"Our mother is fine," Orpah answered. "But, now, are the pots ready?"

"Isn't the shovel too heavy for you?" Ruth asked. "It might be better if my lord or I took them out?"

Orpah shook her head. "No, I can do it. I did it many times when my lord and I — when we —" The ready tears filled her eyes and threatened to overflow.

"It's all right," Ruth said, dreading the tears. It seemed to her that she had done nothing for the past six months except wipe away the tears that Orpah and Naomi shed. It wasn't that she was unsympathetic, she told herself with a twinge of shame. It was just that on such a sunny morning, words were preferable to tears.

Orpah wiped her hands quickly across her cheeks. "Besides," she said, "our mother wants to talk to you, Ruth. She wants to know if you can come over to our house to speak to her."

Ruth looked puzzled. "Is it really necessary? The clay is not quite finished."

Orpah glanced at Mahlon and glanced away again with the same mute embarrassment that Ruth had seen on her husband's face when Orpah came in. There was something going on here that Ruth did not understand.

Mahlon stopped his wheel and stood up. "Go on," he said in a brusque voice. "I'll finish the wedging. If my mother wants to see you, there is no question about the necessity. Go now."

Orpah picked up the broad, short handled shovel that lifted the pots out of the kiln and hurried out into the yard.

For a moment, Ruth stood without moving, her hands chilled and heavy with the wet clay. Then, with a nod of acquiescence toward Mahlon, she wiped the clay from her hands, rinsed them in the basin that stood on the floor, and dried them with a length of cloth kept for that purpose.

"I'll be back as soon as I can," she said.

She started toward the door, but Mahlon stopped her with a gesture.

"My hands are dirty," he said, "and I don't want to touch you. But kiss me before you go."

The request was so wholly unexpected that Ruth was filled with a sudden apprehension. She had been right in thinking that there was something going on.

"My lord," she whispered and lifted her lips to her husband's.

His kiss was gentle and when she looked at him, she saw that his eyes were warm.

"You know you mean much to me," he said. Abruptly, his face changed. "Now go."

Without another word, she hurried toward the house where Orpah and Naomi lived, but her apprehension had not lifted with Mahlon's caress. It had, in fact, only deepened at the unexpectedness of both his kiss and his words. It was not like Mahlon to express his feelings or to show her how he felt.

3

"MOTHER," RUTH CALLED softly as she entered the single room of Chilion's house. Expecting Naomi to be waiting for her, Ruth felt only a sense of bewilderment as she saw the empty room.

Then, faintly, the answer came from the roof. "I'm up here. On the roof. I decided to take advantage of the brightness. Come up, my dear."

Naomi's face was warm with welcome when Ruth joined her. "Thank you for coming, my daughter. Here, come and sit beside me. I want to talk to you."

Ruth felt surprise touch her. Since Chilion's death, Naomi had not indulged in conversation. She had wrapped herself in silence, speaking briefly in greeting or making comment on the task she was doing, but there had been none of the conversations of happier days.

Ruth sat down on the floor beside Naomi and smiled. "I've missed talking with you, Mother," she confided.

Naomi nodded. "You think I don't understand?" she asked. "It's just that my heart has been too heavy for words. And this, today, that I want to talk about — you may not find this pleasant at all."

Ruth only looked at her mother-in-law with a questioning glance and then waited, without comment, until Naomi spoke again.

"In our country," Naomi began, speaking slowly, seeming to have difficulty finding the right words, "we have a law, a custom. It's very important, you see, that children be raised to honor their father."

Ruth felt the familiar pang of guilt and pain. Every time she convinced herself that Naomi was somewhat reconciled to the idea of her childlessness, something was said to prove again that there was no reconciliation at all.

"Mother," Ruth began with breathless apology, but Naomi raised her hand to stop her.

"No, my daughter," Naomi said, "I know your heart yearns for children. I know that. And I don't know why Yahweh has made you barren, but this is just one more sorrow He has given me to bear."

Ruth spoke quickly, suddenly daring to say the words that she had wanted to say for a long time. "How can you honor a god so much when he has done so many cruel things to you?"

Naomi looked astonished. "What has that to do with it?" she asked. "I have no choice. Yahweh created me, just as He created all the world. It's my portion to honor Him."

"When the god, Chemosh, does things I don't understand," Ruth argued, "when he and his consort, Ashtar, command the villagers to get drunk and to do as they do during the fertility rites, I can't possibly honor him. Or when Patima's baby was sacrificed, instead of honoring Chemosh, I almost hated him." It was a confession she had never made to anyone before, and she felt both frightened and relieved.

Naomi gave her a look of compassion. "Of course," she said. "I know about these rites, these orgies. They're disgusting. No wonder you can't honor Chemosh. But Yahweh, now — He is a good and a mighty God, and so I honor Him even when He heaps bitterness and loss on my head."

"But this isn't what you wanted me to come and talk about, is it, Mother?" Ruth asked, uneasy with the turn of the conversation.

"In a way, yes," Naomi answered. "If you don't understand how we feel about our God, you'll never understand what I'm going to say."

"I know that you and my lord submit to your God in all things," Ruth murmured.

"Then you surely know that when He gives us laws to follow, we must obey, even if we're hurt by the act."

Ruth looked puzzled. "What has this to do with me, Mother?"

Naomi took a deep breath and looked up to meet Ruth's eyes. "Yahweh has commanded that fathers be honored, and sometimes this must be done even after a father is dead."

Her voice trembled on the last word, and Ruth waited without speaking.

Naomi picked up the spindle she had laid down, and, keeping her eyes on it, began to speak slowly. "If a man dies, as my son Chilion died, and leaves no sons, then it's the responsibility of his brother to take his widow and raise up sons to the dead man's name."

For a few seconds Ruth sat stunned, feeling her face stiffen with shock. "What do you mean?" she said at last.

Naomi glanced up. "I think you know, my daughter. Orpah has no children to carry on Chilion's name or to carry on Elimelech's name, for that matter. Oh, she bore children easily enough, but they must have been cursed in the womb because they died. Now, if Mahlon who is stronger than Chilion was, took Orpah to wife, if she bore a son, then Chilion's name and my husband's name could be carried on with honor."

"You mean that my lord would divorce me?" Ruth gasped.

Naomi looked shocked. "No, of course not. You and Orpah would both be his wives."

A bitter rejoinder pushed its way out of Ruth's lips before she could stop the words. "I thought *you* were the one who didn't approve of orgies," she said.

Naomi winced as though Ruth had struck her. "How dare you talk so to me?" she whispered. "This isn't like you at all."

"This isn't like you either," Ruth cried. "My lord Mahlon is *my* husband. Haven't I had enough to bear without this added humiliation?"

"Enough to bear?" Naomi asked. "Being married to a foreigner, you mean?"

It was so exactly what Ruth had meant that she could find no words for an answer. She could only sit in silence, staring at her hands, wondering what to do, what to say.

"Mother," she began miserably, "I'm sorry, I —"

Naomi was silent, but Ruth could see the tears that began to slide down Naomi's cheeks.

"Mother, don't cry. I'm sorry. Truly I am. It's just that I hadn't expected anything like this."

"You've always been so obedient before," Naomi murmured, and when Ruth failed to answer she added, "Then you won't permit it?"

"You mean I actually have a choice?"

"Of course. In a sense, you do. Do you think a husband would want to bring quarreling and bitterness into his house? Mahlon said, 'If it cannot be done peacefully —'"

Ruth's hands moved convulsively. "You've already asked him?" she cried.

"Of course," Naomi said again. "There's no one left but him."

The pathos of the last sentence softened Ruth's sense of rebellion. "Well, then — if he wants this thing, what can I say?"

Naomi spoke up quickly. "I know how you feel, honestly I do. I know that you're fond of my son and have been a good and loyal wife —"

"Except for being barren," Ruth interrupted.

"Except for being barren," Naomi agreed. "If you had been able to conceive as Orpah has, then perhaps —" She paused for a moment and then went on almost pleadingly.

"It's because Orpah has no trouble conceiving, don't you understand? Perhaps if Mahlon were the father of her child —"

Ruth felt a great sense of weariness. There was no use arguing with this determined woman. There was no sense in even nurturing the feeling of rebellion that had surged through her when Naomi first made her suggestion. Hadn't she known, since she was a child, that only in obedience could there be peace and contentment for a woman? And hadn't she always known that peace was as much as a woman dared to covet.

"I understand, Mother. The custom seems shocking to me, but if you and my lord have agreed to this thing, then I'll have to accept it."

"Ruth, listen," Naomi urged, "listen to me. Don't be reluctant about it. If you were the one left alone, childless, with no husband, I would have done the same for you. Even though you have never conceived, I would have done the same for you."

"I know. I know, Mother."

"Then you'll be kind to Orpah?"

"Have I ever been anything but kind to her?"

"No," Naomi said, "of course not. But you've never been asked to share your husband with her either."

"You'll have to ask your god to give me strength," Ruth admitted.

"I pray for you every day," Naomi assured her. "Ever since the day my son brought you to our house ten years ago as a bride, I've prayed for you. Why would I stop now?"

"Thank you, Mother," Ruth said, but the words were perfunctory. There was no feeling of gratitude in all the emotions that whirled through her mind. "Is that all you wanted to say to me?"

Naomi drew in a quick breath as though she wanted to say something more, but a sudden call from downstairs interrupted her.

"Mother!" It was Orpah's voice. "Mother, I've finished

taking the pots out of the kiln. Shall I come up to help with the spinning?"

"Does she know?" Ruth whispered.

"I told her I'd try to work it out," Naomi said.

"Why did you come to me last?" Ruth asked in a hot, choking voice, unable to suppress the bitterness that rose in her throat.

Naomi looked suddenly old. "It seemed the right thing to do," she said.

Ruth found herself standing and moving toward the steps. She gave no customary or courteous sign of farewell, and for a second she thought she could not. But the habit of obedience was strong, stronger than the anger in her. She turned to Naomi. "Will you excuse me, Mother? I have work to do in the shop."

If I were a man, Ruth thought in despair, if I were a man, I would leave this rooftop and go so far away that no one in this village would ever see me again. Not my husband, nor the neighbors who will gossip about this thing, nor this woman who thinks that her god gives her the right to plan my life, nor Orpah, nor...But I am not a man, she reflected bleakly.

Somehow, she smiled at Naomi. "Whenever you need me, Mother."

Some of the age drained out of Naomi's face. Her lips were pale, but she returned Ruth's smile. "You're a good girl," she said. "A good girl."

Ruth walked slowly down the steps. Orpah was waiting at the bottom. What will I see in her eyes? Ruth wondered. Will she be happy and proud, even haughty?

"Ruth," Orpah said, and Ruth turned reluctantly to face her. "Ruth, listen." There was no victory in her eyes. "It's as hard for me as it is for you. Chilion was my husband. I don't want — I don't think —" Her voice trailed off.

"I was just thinking of how I felt," Ruth confessed.

Orpah nodded. "I know. I wish things were different. But Naomi is our mother and I know she loves you."

"She loves you, you mean," Ruth argued.

Orpah shook her head. "No," she said. "I'm only some-one who might be able to bear a child."

What Orpah said might be true, Ruth thought, but it didn't make Naomi's suggestion any easier to accept.

"Whether she cares more for you or for me doesn't matter," Ruth said. "But what she's asking us to do will take time to get used to." She hesitated. "How soon do they —"

"Not right away," Orpah answered. "I told her I couldn't, not right away."

Ruth hadn't believed, talking to Naomi, that Orpah would ever be her ally. Up there on the roof, she had begun to think of Orpah as the enemy. Now she saw how wrong she had been.

"Thank you," Ruth said. Impulsively, she bent and kissed Orpah's cheek. "Maybe something will happen so it won't even be necessary."

"If my father would come and insist on finding me another husband," Orpah murmured. "But he won't. He's had six daughters to marry off. It was why he married me to a foreigner in the first place."

"Still," Ruth said, "there's always a chance."

She hurried out of the small house and stood for a minute in the yard, drawing deep breaths of the clear, sparkling air. It was hard to believe that only a few hours ago she had looked up at the sky with delight, finding joy in the day.

Mahlon was waiting for her, his usually placid face taut with worry.

"Are you all right?" he asked.

She wanted to cry out that she wasn't all right, that she might very well never be all right again. She wanted to shed the tears that ached behind her eyes. But she knew that Mahlon had grown as weary of tears as she had.

"Yes, my lord," she said and looked away from him. "I'm all right."

"If it happens," Mahlon said, his voice rough, "it will be simply a thing done out of duty and obedience to our law. She won't take your place with me."

There was no reassurance in Mahlon's words. It seemed to Ruth that there was nothing in her life to comfort her, not even Mahlon's rare assurance of his affection.

"Let me finish the wedging," she said with such force in her voice that Mahlon moved aside without a word.

She plunged her hands into the clay, finding a curious release for her tension in the working of the resistant stuff.

"Don't beat it to death," Mahlon said in his mild voice, and she looked up to find him watching her, his eyes amused.

She had thought she would never smile again, and it was true, as she had said to Patima, that there was little in this house to laugh at. And yet, here was Mahlon on the verge of laughter.

"It's good to know a wife can be jealous," he said. "Some women wouldn't even have cared."

She stared in astonishment. "Jealous, my lord?"

"What else?"

What else indeed?

Reluctantly, her lips curved. "It's just that Orpah is so small and pretty," she admitted.

"She's like a child," Mahlon said. "Haven't I ever told you I was glad when my father said you were tall? Haven't I ever told you I liked a woman who looked like a woman?"

"No, my lord, you've never told me."

"Well, I've told you now," he said. "As soon as that clay is ready, call me and I'll start to work with it. I'll go out and see to the clay in the yard."

"Be careful," she said, but she said it automatically. "You know how slippery it is. Don't fall." She said the words every time, but she was sure that he didn't even hear her.

Today, however, he said, "I'll be careful." His smile was warm.

She watched him leave the shop. In all their ten years together, she had never felt so close to him before. He may not truly love me, she thought, but he has come closer to it than I ever thought an Israelite could.

4

"IS SOMETHING THE MATTER?" Patima's voice was shrewd. She and Ruth were walking toward the well, and a thin, cold rain wet their heads and faces even though they had pulled their scarves nearly down to their eyes. "You've looked different lately. Is something wrong?"

Ruth shook her head, but Patima persisted.

"Is your lord still angry because I insisted on paying for the jar? He wouldn't be so foolish, would he?"

"He's proud," Ruth said. "His pride was hurt."

"Pride never filled an empty belly," Patima said.

"A man has to have something to help him keep his head up," Ruth argued. "I don't mean I think he was right. I understand how he felt, though."

"It's not fair that he should have to support two families," Patima protested. "Is that what's wrong with you, then? You're angry, too?

"How could I be angry with your kindness?" Ruth cried. "No, I'm not angry. It's — " A dozen times during the past days she had longed to talk to Patima about Naomi's suggestion, but some stiff loyalty had kept her silent.

"What?" There was no mischief in Patima's eyes, only concern, reminding Ruth of their childhood when Patima had protected her against the other children. "You look older all at once. And worried. Is there anything I can do?"

34

"No," Ruth said, "there's nothing anyone can do."

Patima spoke with decisiveness. "Look, if we walk straight to the well, there will be others there. Let's walk around the long way as we used to before we were married. Then we can talk." She hesitated briefly. "You do want to talk, don't you?"

"Yes," Ruth admitted in a whisper. "I need to talk to someone."

Patima made a sound of satisfaction. "Then let's go down this way."

"But it's raining," Ruth protested. "We can wait until some morning when it's dry."

"We won't melt," Patima said. "Come on."

Ruth turned obediently, and for a few minutes they walked in silence.

"Well?" Patima prodded.

"I don't even know how to start," Ruth said, her voice helpless and tired. "But my mother-in-law has asked me to let my husband take Orpah to wife."

Patima stopped and stared at Ruth in horror. "Divorce you, you mean?"

"No, it's not like that at all." Stumbling over the words, stopping often to find the right ones, Ruth poured out her strange little story.

"That's crazy," Patima said.

"It's the way they do it in Israel," Ruth answered.

"But they're not in Israel. They're in Moab."

"Nevertheless — "

The two women walked on in silence. Ruth felt the rain sliding across her face and it seemed to her as though her whole world were weeping.

When Patima spoke again, her voice had lost its bewilderment and shock and was once again brisk and practical.

"Well, then, I guess you'll have to do it."

Ruth stopped as though she had been struck. "That's the only answer you have for me?"

"What did you expect, my sister? A miracle?"

Ruth walked on blindly, more upset by Patima's instant acceptance of the situation than she had been by Naomi's proposal.

"Listen," Patima said, "if you fight them, if you object, what will you gain? Only their anger. You will have gained only two enemies. Would it be worth it?"

Ruth thought of the fantasies that had filled her waking and sleeping hours, fantasies in which Orpah had found a wealthy husband who would take her away. In the light of Patima's simple practicality, she saw how foolish they had been.

Patima's voice went on. "Naomi loves you and is kinder to you than most mothers-in-law are. You should have to listen to my mother-in-law sometimes. Even in front of me, she tells my husband what a wicked and lazy girl I am. And Mahlon — isn't he good to you? Has he ever spoken of divorcing you even though there are no children?"

It was hard for Ruth to speak, and her voice came out hoarsely. "No, he's better than I deserve, I know. And Naomi, well, I've always loved her, only — "

"Only now she's asking something of you that you're not willing to give," Patima said. "So you've quit loving her. Is that it?"

The plain, sharp words stung Ruth. "No," she cried. I haven't stopped loving her. It's just — "

"Just what? Are you jealous of the thought of Orpah sharing your husband?"

"Wouldn't you be?" Ruth retorted.

"Of course. But, I'd rather share him than have no one."

Ruth did not answer for several minutes. The rain continued to fall lightly, but she hardly felt it. She remembered Mahlon's face when he had said, "Didn't I ever tell you I was glad when my father said you were tall?" He had looked young, his eyes warm.

Patima spoke again, her words almost harsh. "What do you expect? Do you expect your life to be a love story — you who are married to a foreigner and who have no children?"

Ruth made a sudden sound of pain, and Patima put a gentle hand on her arm. "I'm not being cruel. I'm looking at your life honestly. You're a good woman and a beautiful one, even though you might seem too tall for some men." She hesitated and then said very softly, "Are you afraid he'll be smitten with Orpah's looks?"

"He told me he liked tall women," Ruth confessed.

"Since all this happened, he told you that?"

Ruth nodded.

"Well, then," Patima said, obviously relaxing. "You've got nothing to worry about. He'll still be fond of you and take care of you. That's what matters. Have you ever thought of how it is for women who have no husband, no sons? You don't really have any choice, Ruth. You're silly to grieve."

Her sister was right, Ruth knew. Patima had always been the practical, the sensible one. Patima had never longed for the moon. Patima had been content with her daily bread. Then why is it different for me? Ruth wondered.

"The neighbors will gossip," Ruth said suddenly.

"Of course they will," Patima agreed. "Does that bother you so much?"

Ruth remembered the other times she had been the object of gossip — when she had first been married to an Israelite, when she had refused to take part in the wild revelry of the followers of Chemosh. But she had not minded because she had felt supported by Naomi and Mahlon, even Orpah and Chilion. Now she was alone.

Or was she? "Did I ever tell you," Mahlon had said, "that I like a woman who looks like a woman?" And "You're a good girl," Naomi had said. "A good girl." No, she wasn't alone. Things might not be just what she wanted but she wouldn't be alone.

"I expect I could survive gossip," Ruth said. "Will you defend me?"

For the first time that morning, Patima's eyes twinkled in

the old familiar way. "I'll say, 'What can you expect of foreigners? My poor sister had no choice.' They'll come to sympathize in the end. You'll see."

Ruth tried to smile. "I don't know what I'd do without you," she admitted.

"Well, you don't have to worry," Patima said. "I don't plan to leave town."

They had come, in their round-about way, to the area of the well. More people were milling around than usual, and Ruth was aware of an air of excitement or confusion.

"I wonder what's happened," she said. "Everyone seems to be running around in circles."

"The children," Patima exclaimed. "If my mother-in-law has let anything happen to the children — "

"There's Orpah," Ruth said. "She'll know."

At that moment, Orpah turned and saw Ruth and Patima hurrying toward the well. "Ruth," she cried, her voice shrill and breathless, "Ruth, we've been looking for you. Hurry. Mahlon has fallen and hit his head. Oh, hurry."

Ruth felt a coldness fill her, so that she faltered in her running. Her legs felt too heavy to move. "Oh, no," she whispered.

Patima lifted Ruth's water jar out of her hands and pushed her sharply. "Don't stand there. Run."

The impact of Patima's shove and the sharpness of her words released Ruth from her momentary immobility. Without a word or a look at Patima or anyone else, she started running toward home. Orpah tried to keep up with her, but it was as though Ruth had wings. Silently she raced along the street while a single thought kept repeating itself through her mind. If I had been home instead of out walking with Patima, I would have warned him. I would have told him to be careful. It's my fault...my fault...

Naomi crouched beside Mahlon, rocking back and forth in silent agony. Ruth, gasping for breath, dropped down beside her, staring with horror at the gray, still face of her husband.

"My lord," she whispered, "Oh, my lord, are you all right?"

Naomi's tears fell like the morning rain, making clean streaks on Mahlon's muddy feet. She made no effort to touch her son or speak to him. She only rocked back and forth in her dreadful, soundless grief.

Ruth was aware that Orpah had come into the small room.

"What happened?" Ruth cried. "What happened to him?"

"He went out to get clay," Orpah panted. "He must have slipped. Even in our house I heard the sound of his head hitting the little stone wall around the clay. I ran out at once, but he never spoke. Mother and I carried him into the house."

I wasn't even here, Ruth grieved. I should have been the one who carried him in. I should have been here to tell him to be careful. He was always careless about the clay.

"The rain made it more slippery than usual," Orpah said. "I don't really know what happened."

"We need a priest," Naomi shrilled. "We need a priest of Yahweh."

Ruth looked up, remembering how Naomi had cried these same words during Chilion's illness and at his death. "Mother, there are no priests of Yahweh here. You know that."

"We should never have left Israel," Naomi wailed. "We should never have come to this place. Oh, Yahweh, my God, what should I do?"

"There are priests of Chemosh," Orpah suggested timidly.

Before Naomi could answer, Ruth spoke bitterly. "And what could they do, those priests? What do they know of such an accident as this?"

"When my grandfather hit his head, they opened the swelling, and they — " Orpah began.

"Did they make him well?" Ruth demanded.

"No, he — he died," Orpah faltered.

"You see?" Ruth dismissed the priests of Chemosh with a gesture of scorn. But at the same time, her heart was crying out with panic, What shall we do? Who can help us?

"Get some water," Ruth said in desperation. "Please, Orpah, find a cloth and some water. I'll wipe his face and — don't mothers put cool cloths on a child's head when he falls?"

"What good will a cloth do?" Naomi wept. "Are you blind, girl? Can't you see he's dead?"

Ruth rounded on Naomi in horror. "Don't *say* that! He can't be dead. He only slipped and fell. A man doesn't die because he falls in the mud."

Naomi stared at her with wild eyes. "Does he breathe?" she asked. "Tell me, does he breathe?"

Ruth tore her eyes from Naomi's and stared down at Mahlon. Of course he was breathing. He had to be breathing. Wouldn't she know if he were dead?

She leaned closer to him, trying to see clearly in spite of the fact that her eyes were blurred with tears. Of course he was gray and still, but he was unconscious from the blow. Only unconscious.

She put her hand on his face and the chill of his flesh ran up her arm. She leaned closer, straining to see some movement of his chest, to feel some air from his lips.

It was Orpah's hand that pulled her back.

"No, my sister," Orpah said, her voice shaking. "She's right. Our mother is right. Your lord is dead."

"My God, my God," Naomi wept and huddled close to Mahlon's feet, not touching him but unable to move away from him.

"No," Ruth cried, stunned. "He's only hurt. He's only unconscious from the fall. He can't be dead."

But she did not try to touch him again. Her body seemed to know instinctively what her mind could not accept.

All three women continued to kneel beside Mahlon's body, none of them able to run for help. Naomi wept and rocked back and forth, and Orpah sobbed in a despairing way. But Ruth was quiet, incapable of sound or motion.

"I'll call someone," Orpah said at last, and turned to run from the room. It was as though her departure released something that had been holding Ruth immobile and silent. With a sudden wild cry, Ruth reached for Mahlon with yearning hands.

"Don't touch him!" Naomi commanded sharply. "Don't touch him."

"But he's my husband," Ruth cried.

"And he's my son," Naomi whispered.

Her quietness stopped Ruth's mounting hysteria. Turning, she met Naomi's eyes and saw the desolation in them.

"Oh, Mother," Ruth said brokenly. "Oh, Mother, I need you."

Naomi reached out to Ruth with a sob. "My child, my child. You're all I have left."

They held each other, first in silence, then with a mounting crescendo of grief. Neither of them knew whether she was supporting or being supported. But each knew, even in her pain, that without the other, she would have fallen into darkness.

5

PATIMA WAS THE FIRST to arrive. She came in quickly, and when she saw Ruth and Naomi clinging together, weeping, she cried out in a voice of horror, "Truly he's not dead?"

Ruth looked up. Even now the word seemed incredible, unbearable. Dumbly she nodded. Patima cast herself down beside her sister, and for a few minutes her shrill cries climbed over Naomi's hoarse weeping.

"Alas, my brother," Patima wept, rocking back and forth. "Alas, my brother."

Almost immediately, other people began to crowd into the room. Ruth's and Orpah's family came to see, to pity and to mourn.

At least, Ruth thought with a dull sense of appreciation, we won't have to hire professional mourners. With all of these friends and relatives to weep, we won't have to hire the singing women to come in.

As though Ruth's thoughts had prompted her, Naomi lifted her head abruptly. "Wait," she called out, "he isn't prepared for death yet, this son of mine. Will you leave my son's wife and me alone with him for a little while? When he's ready for your tears, then we'll welcome you. And will one of you call the singing women? My son must be given every honor. Even though he's a stranger in a land of strangers."

Her voice was high and breaking, but she had overcome her first hysteria. Ruth, seeing Naomi's strength, pushed her own terror and shock into the back of her mind. She knew they could not afford to hire the professional mourners, but since Naomi had already announced her desire to have them, it would be foolish to try to dissuade her.

Most of the people moved out of the room, but Ruth was aware of the presence of Patima and Orpah and her mother as she began the ritual tasks. She had thought only a few minutes ago that she could not touch Mahlon's body, but now she realized that it was simply something that had to be done. With gentle hands, she straightened his robe, tucking it neatly under him and pulling it up around his throat. She washed his hands and feet and the ugly wound on his head, rinsing away the clay and blood. Then she crossed his hands, pulling his sleeves down to his wrists as though she were afraid he would be cold.

Patima handed her the long robe of cotton which had been Mahlon's best one, and Ruth wrapped it closely around his body. When she had to lift him to get the cloth under him, it was Patima who helped her. Naomi and Orpah had resumed their bitter weeping, content to let Ruth and Patima arrange the body for burial.

When the task was finished, Ruth continued to kneel wearily beside her husband. Leaning forward, she kissed his forehead, feeling the chill hardness of the flesh under her lips.

In that instant, her strength fled, and she crouched over Mahlon's body, sobbing desperately. Almost at once, the room was filled with mourners, and the sound of wailing and of ripping cloth filled the air.

The professional mourners came very soon after that, and Ruth shuddered away from the shrill, harsh sound of their cries. From the time she was small, she had been terrified by the wild looks and sounds of the singing women. The sight of the torn hair, the lacerated flesh, the ashes streaking down the tear-wet faces had always frightened her, but if they brought comfort to Naomi, then it was enough. As for herself, nothing could comfort her.

Patima's hand on her arm finally caught her attention. "Could I speak to you?" Patima whispered.

Ruth nodded and got up from the ground. They moved toward the door and stepped out into the damp, fresh air. The daylight fell with pain across Ruth's tear-blind eyes.

"I've spoken to my lord Faran," Patima said in a low voice. "When the mourners first came, I slipped out and found him. He's willing that Mahlon should be buried in our cave."

"My husband was no relation to Faran's father and his ancestors," Ruth cried. "Why would your lord be so generous to us?"

"Your father-in-law had to be buried in a trench in the ground with only stones piled over him to keep the wild animals away," Orpah said. "And little better was done for Chilion. But that was because no one in Bezer really knew Elimelech when he died and Orpah's family had no room in their cave for Chilion."

She paused and put her hand on Ruth's arm. "It's different with Mahlon. He's — he was — married to one of our family. My lord Faran wants to give him a burial place."

"It would comfort me more than anything in the world," Ruth admitted. "But will my mother-in-law permit it? She still thinks of us as pagan."

"Ask her," Patima urged. "Ask her and remind her of the danger of jackals. If she won't permit it, then we'll have to have a grave dug in the earth. But if she'll permit it, my lord will start having the cave opened up."

"I'll ask her," Ruth agreed.

It was difficult to get Naomi's attention. Her mourning had disintegrated into bitterness, and she was rocking back and forth, railing at her God who had allowed this incredible disaster to fall into her life.

Ruth finally persuaded Naomi to come away from the mourners, to listen to Patima's offer. At first, Naomi only shook her head, saying over and over, "He should be buried with his father and his brother, with a priest of Yahweh to chant a prayer."

"But there are no priests," Ruth repeated patiently. "And his father's grave has long been covered over by blowing soil. You know that, Mother. We're not even sure exactly where it is. Wouldn't it be better to have Mahlon's body safe from the animals? It's really very good of Faran to offer the cave."

She said the same words at least half a dozen times before Naomi acted as though she were really listening. Finally, the older woman began to nod in agreement.

"It's true I had Mahlon and Chilion to dig a deep grave when my lord Elimelech died," she whispered at last. "And now there is no one."

"My brother-in-law and his friends will carry Mahlon to the cave," Ruth said. "We'll never have to worry about jackals. He'll be placed in a safe, dry place."

Naomi's only response was to bury her face in her hands and weep again, but Ruth knew the lack of real opposition indicated consent. Gently leading Naomi back to the center of the room, she turned to find her sister.

"Please tell your lord," she said, "that we'll be grateful for his kindness. Tell him — " But her voice broke and she could say no more.

"The men will come soon," Patima promised. "The body will be buried before sundown. You won't have to worry."

Almost too soon, it seemed to Ruth, several men came to the door. Without speaking, they entered the room and lifted Mahlon's body to carry it out of the room.

"My son, my son." Naomi wailed and reached for him with yearning hands.

Ruth was so intent on calming the older woman, so concerned about holding the groping hands safely in her own, so anxious that Naomi be spared that last sad sight of her son that she was almost unaware of her own pain.

"Here, Mother," she begged, "let me hold you. Here, put

your head on my shoulder. Let me hold your hands. There, there," as though she were talking to a very small child, "don't weep so, you'll be sick. Sit here, Mother, here where there's a little breeze from the door."

Half fainting, her cries diminished to moans, Naomi let Ruth lead her to the doorway and sat her with her back against the wall. Pulling her veil across her face, she leaned her head back and sat in stillness.

Ruth looked around her dazedly. The body was gone. Mahlon was gone. The shock of loss daggered through her, but she found some slight comfort in the fact that her sister's family had taken him in. In death, at least, there had been some gesture of friendship toward the foreigner in their midst.

Well, there was no point in even thinking about it. The seven days of mourning and fasting were still to be endured. And soon enough, when the formal mourning period was behind them, they were going to have to find a way for three widows to survive with no sons to care for them.

On the eighth day after Mahlon's death, Ruth woke up with a strange feeling of relief. It was not, she told herself, that she wanted to stop grieving for Mahlon. It was just that it was not her nature to share her sorrow so blatantly, to express her hurt to everyone around her. The tears she shed at night, she reflected, were the true tears. The public mourning during the day seemed to come easily for Orpah and Naomi, but Ruth had endured it with a mixture of shyness and shame.

I'm too private a person for this, she thought, and knew that privacy was something she might never have again. The fasting had been easy, because food seemed to stick in her throat. After sundown each day, when neighbors brought food, Naomi and Orpah had broken their fast, as was customary, but Ruth had been unable to eat. That much of it had been real, not show.

But now the specified seven days were past. We can get on with living, Ruth thought gratefully when she woke up. I can start to plan our lives and try to figure out what we're going to do.

She went quietly to the pottery and stood looking around the empty room. At first, her eyes blurred with tears, but she shook her head with anger. Tears solved nothing.

Perhaps I could make pots, she thought. I watched Mahlon and Chilion enough times. I may have been awkward when I was first married and all thumbs the time Mahlon let me try, but I know much more about the clay now. I've wedged it and I know the feel of it. I've tramped out the moisture and I know the proper texture. I've watched Mahlon's fingers shaping the coils, piling them, smoothing them. If I tried, I could do it now.

The clay was still damp in its bin, because even in the midst of sorrowing, she had daily replenished the wet cloths. She took out a mass of the clay, threw it on the table and began the familiar task of wedging. Just seven days away from the work had weakened her hands and arms and shoulders, so that she found the clay more resistant and stubborn than ever.

Before she finished, Naomi and Orpah had come to find her. They stood watching her, weeping their easy tears.

"How can you even touch the clay, my sister?" Orpah wept.

"Because," Ruth said grimly, "we have to eat. We have to have something to trade for food. The harvest season won't come for many months yet — not until the end of spring, and it's still winter. We have to eat."

She began the kneading process again, feeling pain across her shoulders and up into her neck.

"We can't make pots," Naomi said. "You know we can't."

"Maybe because we've never tried," Ruth grated. "Maybe we just think we can't. I have to try."

"The wheel is hard to turn," Naomi protested. "Your legs won't be strong enough."

"I have to try," Ruth repeated and kept her head bent, so that she would not have to see Naomi's doubt and Orpah's despair.

"There's no use treading more clay until you see if you can really make pots," Naomi decided at last. "Orpah and I will go to the well."

So Ruth was alone when she finally sat down on Mahlon's seat by the potter's wheel. She shaped the clay into coils, making them as close to the size Mahlon had made as she could. The treadle moved stiffly, resistantly under her feet, and before she had the first coil shaped into the bottom of a pot, her legs were starting to ache. But she kept at it doggedly, looping, patting, smoothing, wetting her hands and wetting the clay.

Nothing went right. One coil slid off the one beneath it, bulges protruded from the rounded sides of the growing pot.

Stubbornly, Ruth persisted. By the time Orpah and Naomi came back there was only a tortured lump of clay on the slowly rotating stone wheel. Hot and cross and frustrated, Ruth glared at the other two women.

"Go ahead, say it!" she snapped. "Tell me that you were right, and I was wrong. Tell me I'm stupid and clumsy. Go ahead."

Naomi shrugged, and for the first time since Mahlon died, a small smile lifted her lips from their curve of sorrow. "It's not very pretty," Naomi agreed, "but it's true you had to try."

Ruth's exasperation and anger suddenly drained away. Unexpectedly, she began to laugh. "Did you ever see such a mess in all your life?" she demanded ruefully. "I tried to move my fingers exactly the way my lord did, and I made the kind of mud cakes a child would make. Just look at it."

Orpah giggled. "It would take us a year of daily trials before we learned to make even the simplest pots. And no one wants that. People want the kind of things Mahlon and my lord Chilion made."

"So." Naomi's voice was suddenly brisk and practical. "So what do we do now?"

Ruth gathered up the clay from her pathetic attempts and threw it back into the bin. The very act of flinging the clay was a curious release, and she was still smiling when she went to wash her hands.

"We'll have to find a potter," Naomi said.

"What good will that do us?" Ruth asked. "If a potter comes, he'll have a family and the business can't support — oh! you mean, sell the business to him."

"Maybe. We do have two houses, you know. We three could move into Mahlon's house, and then we'd have a house and a business to bargain with."

Ruth nodded. It had never occurred to her that she would be allowed to stay on in her house alone, so she felt no real disappointment.

"But where will we find a potter?" Orpah asked. "There are none here in Bezer. That's why Israelites were welcome in this town — because they had a skill that was needed in Bezer."

"Still," Ruth said, "Mother's right. We have to find a potter. The word will get around. There are always men who go from village to village trading or buying. Word will get around."

"In the meantime," Naomi said, "Ruth is the one who's right. We must get to work. We must try. We'll start by moving into Mahlon's house. It will take us a while. We'll scrub and clean Chilion's house so that the place will be ready."

The three women were silent for a minute, and Ruth finally spoke. "It will be good to work, Mother. There's healing in work. I feel it already, even though I ruined the pot."

Naomi nodded. "This is something women know, I think. All women — Israelite or Moabite. We can grieve only so long, and then we have to start to work. It's the way Yahweh made us."

It's the way Yahweh made *you*, Ruth thought. I'm a Moabite. But she knew, from talks she had shared with her mother-in-law, that Naomi believed that Yahweh had made all creatures, all land and sea. Ruth neither agreed nor disagreed. She simply didn't know. She only knew that she rather envied Naomi's unquestioning faith, but she was much too shy to question her mother-in-law about the way such faith could be learned.

6

THE LAST COAT of whitewash was completely applied, and Ruth stood looking at the walls of Chilion's house with an immense sense of satisfaction. Faran had provided the whitewash, and when Ruth had tried to thank him, he had waved her thanks away.

"It's to my own advantage," he had said, grinning. "First, if we can find a potter, you'll be taken care of, you and Orpah and the Israelite woman, and I won't have to worry about it any longer. What's more, my wife will stop nagging me."

Ruth smiled, remembering. She doubted that Patima really nagged. On the other hand, she would not hesitate to try to persuade her husband to do what she wanted.

It's partly because she's so frank and outspoken, Ruth thought. I wish I were more like that. I wish I trusted people enough to say the way I really feel. But I suppose nothing will ever change me.

Orpah appeared in the door. "It looks nice, doesn't it?" she asked wistfully. Although the two houses were exactly alike, Ruth could understand Orpah's regret at leaving this one which had sheltered her during the years of her marriage.

Ruth smiled at her sister-in-law. "Yes. Very nice. You kept it so clean that getting it ready was really no problem after your things were moved out."

They looked around the small room, letting their gaze rest briefly on the familiar items — the narrow window high in the rear wall, the wooden platform, raised a little above the floor, that held the sleeping mats at night, the round clay oven with its opening on the top on which to set a cooking pot. All the personal things that made a house home-like were gone. Orpah's spindle, the pots of grain or oil, the rolled mats that served as beds had all been carried over to the other house. Only the oven had been left, because it had been made a permanent part of the earthen floor in that corner, and the small lamp, also fashioned of clay which burned continuously on its shelf.

"We must remember to put oil in the lamp," Ruth said absently and looked up at the heavy sycamore logs that stretched across the low ceiling. Smaller logs rested cross-wise on top of the heavy beams and above them was the thick roof of brush and mud. "I cleaned out any insect nests I could find," she went on. "I think even the roof will be all right."

"Mahlon rolled it after the last rains," Orpah offered. "He kept it in good repair after — after my lord Chilion died."

But Ruth would not allow herself to be drawn into that kind of conversation. "Then it'll be up to the new potter, if we ever find one, to keep it in good repair from now on," she said. "Come, there's nothing more to do here."

"Nor in the other house either," Orpah said. "Mother and I have put everything away."

"We might as well go up to the roof to spin," Ruth said. "Has anyone gone for water?"

"I brought home one jar, I don't think we'll need any more today."

They walked out of the little house together, pulling the rude wooden door shut. The place would stay empty until they found a tenant.

And how desperately they needed one, Ruth reflected later in the day, as she made flat loaves of bread for their evening meal. The pot out of which she had scooped the meal had been perilously close to empty, and there was only one more storage jar full of wheat. Even the oil was disappearing too rapidly for comfort. When Chilion and Mahlon were alive, the disappearance of food had never been a problem. There had always been someone eager to obtain pots, willing to bring grain or oil or fruit or vegetables for trade.

And who is there to turn to, Ruth asked herself while her hands patted and shaped the loaves. No one. Oh, Patima would give me of their store, I know she would. Even my father, although he would grumble about it, would give me food if we were hungry. Or perhaps Orpah's family. But no one in this village is rich, no one has great stores of grain and oil. Not at this season of the year when the harvest is still months away. I don't know how we're going to manage. I really don't.

Several weeks later, a man approached their house. Ruth and Naomi, spinning on the roof, saw him coming, and they hurried down the stone steps that climbed up the outside of the house, so that they might meet their visitor outside their door. It would never do for three women alone to invite a stranger into their home.

The man was small, bandy legged, narrow across the shoulders, but he walked with a jaunty, cocky stride, as though trying to atone for his size.

"Welcome," Naomi said when he came close enough for conversation. "The peace of Yahweh be with you."

The man squinted in the sun. "Greetings," he answered. "Are you Naomi, the widow of the Israelite potter?"

"I am. How do you know of me?"

The man looked around as if he were seeking a place to sit, and Ruth waved a hand to indicate the stones that formed a sort of bench near the doorway. He seated himself, smoothing his robe across his knees with a nervous gesture, and then peered up at the two women.

"I heard about you from several people. Everyone seems to know that you need a potter."

Ruth's heart jumped with a sudden stab of excitement. True, the man was unprepossessing, but if he were a potter —

Naomi seated herself near her guest, and Ruth hurried to get a skin of wine and a few dried dates. She offered them, and the man helped himself greedily.

"You're a potter?" Naomi asked. "And your name?"

"My name is Ishbal," he said. "I'm a potter as was my father before me."

"You're not from Bezer?" Naomi's question was delicate, avoiding a direct query.

"No." He offered no other information. "Do you plan to sell the business? What about a house? What are you asking for payment?"

Naomi looked quickly at Ruth. They had decided that if the right man came, they would sell the house and the pottery, hoping to get enough silver or copper to last them for many years.

But if the man were not "right?" They had not discussed this possibility at all. Ruth felt uneasy about the slight, shifty eyed man who sat facing them, but there was no chance to discuss it with Naomi.

It was with a real sense of relief that Ruth heard Naomi say, "We haven't decided. We thought it might be wise to rent the place first. To see how it would work out. There's a house for the potter's use, and we could share in the sale of the pottery, we thought."

Ishbal frowned and turned away to spit on the ground. "I had counted on owning the property," he said sullenly.

"If it all works out well, there's no reason why you wouldn't someday," Naomi said easily. "But the business was my husband's and my son's. I can't dispose of it lightly."

"How do you have the right to dispose of it at all?" Ishbal demanded. "A woman. The business goes to a son, a brother, even a cousin. But always a man."

"My husband is dead." Naomi's voice was cold. "And my sons are both dead. I have no grandsons, nor any kin at all in this country. My husband's family is still in Bethlehem, in Judea."

"It's an unusual situation," Ishbal admitted.

They sat in silence.

"Have you no family, no wife, no children?" Ruth asked, speaking for the first time since Ishbal's arrival.

He shot a quick look at her. "My wife died. I had no children."

Ruth felt a stir of pity. She understood completely the grief that could be hidden in that bald statement.

"Well," Naomi's voice was very practical, "still you have to have a place to live. Even with no wife or children, you have to have a place to sleep, a roof to shelter you from winter rain. And if you're a potter, then you need a pottery."

Ishbal glanced over at the small building that stood between the two houses. "May I see it?" he asked.

"Of course. Come, Ruth, we'll show him where everything is."

Ishbal eyed the younger woman. "Ruth? You're not an Israelite then?"

"I'm a Moabite. This town is my home."

"But you were married to an Israelite?"

Ruth's chin went up. She was remembering with what delicacy Naomi had worded her question. "I was married to Naomi's son, Mahlon."

Ishbal only nodded, letting his eyes flick once more over her face. "Then, come," he said. "Let me see the house and the pottery. Have you a good source of clay?"

"Good enough," Naomi said. "Here, we have this pit in the yard in addition to many larger pits outside the town."

Ruth kept her eyes away from the low stone wall that enclosed the clay pit. She had never been able to really look at it since the day Mahlon had fallen.

Ishbal followed the two women from pit to kiln, from pottery to house, asking questions, examining, studying.

He seems to know what he's talking about, Ruth

thought. He certainly is familiar with all the steps of pottery making, all the needed equipment. His face had brightened at the sight of the pottery, the sturdy wheel, the bin of clay under the wet cloth.

"But you won't sell it outright?" the man asked.

"Not now. Not until I'm sure."

"I have some silver," Ishbal offered.

"Then you'll still have it if I decide to sell." Naomi's voice was abrupt.

He looked angry, but he kept his voice smooth. "Well, then, shall we say that you can have half of the pots I make? They'll serve as rent for the house and pottery. You can sell or trade them."

Ruth caught Naomi's eyes. Don't let him off too easy, she thought, and wondered if her mother-in-law could see the caution in her face.

"Yes," Naomi said slowly, "provided, of course, that you produce enough pots. I wouldn't want to say just any number of pots would be enough."

Ishbal's eyes flicked from one woman to the other. "Have you had other potters consider the business?" he asked.

"No," Naomi admitted. "Not yet."

"Nor likely to," Ishbal said smoothly. "A man works for his father or the man who has apprenticed him. And men stay in their own village. You're lucky to have me."

The terrible part of it, Ruth thought, was that Ishbal was right.

"Still," Naomi said, her voice stubborn, "we'll insist that you do the work properly."

"Don't worry." The words were as smooth as oil. "I'm a good man. A hard worker. You won't need to worry."

"And you can start soon? You won't have to travel home to make any arrangements?" Naomi's questions were still subtle.

"I'm here to stay. I can move into the house today."

Orpah, who had gone to her mother's house, came into

the yard, and Ruth saw the sudden interest on Ishbal's face. "Your daughter?" he said to Naomi.

"My daughter-in-law."

"Also a widow?"

"Also a widow."

"Widow of your older son, perhaps?"

Naomi stared unwaveringly at the man. "Widow of my younger son. Ruth was the wife of my older son, the son who owned the pottery after his father died."

"Oh." Ishbal looked at Ruth appraisingly.

Was that disappointment she saw in his face, she wondered. Whatever it was, the man made her uncomfortable.

"My bundle of belongings is down in the village," Ishbal offered. "I'll go after it now."

"Yes. Fine." Naomi seemed uncertain about what to do or say next.

But Ishbal, still with that jaunty, cocky step, hurried from the yard, almost running toward the village.

"I'm not wholly satisfied," Naomi said. "For all his talk about buying, I'm sure he'll try to get the pottery in some other way. What do *you* think?"

Ruth hesitated a moment before answering. She was far from satisfied, but the man was right when he pointed out that they really had no choice. There was no point in stirring up trouble. "I think you were right to take him on a trial basis," she said cautiously. "Who knows? Some kinsman of your husband's may come one day from Bethlehem, and you might want him to have the business."

"Small chance of that," Naomi said. "Elimelech had kinsmen, of course — potters among them, I'm sure — but it's as this Ishbal says, if a man has a pottery business, he's not apt to leave his own village."

"Well, we'll have to try it," Ruth said. "Nothing can be certain until we've tried."

Orpah had stood in silence during the entire conversation. When she finally spoke, her voice was hard and uncompromising. "He makes my flesh crawl," she stated baldly. "The thought of him handling the tools that my lord Chilion used makes my flesh crawl."

Naomi stared in astonishment at the younger woman. She opened her mouth as though to protest but then closed it again. After a few seconds, she shrugged her shoulders and spread her hands in a gesture of helplessness. "We have to eat, don't we?" she asked reasonably. "The grain is disappearing and the oil is nearly gone. A woman has to make compromises if she's going to survive."

"I suppose." Orpah's voice was sullen. She looked across at Ruth. "Do you like him?" she asked.

Ruth tried to laugh. "I don't even know him, and besides, as Mother says, what difference does it make? We've found a potter, and we'll have to make do with that."

"It's my own fault," Naomi said suddenly, her voice very clear and sharp. "I left it up to luck. I didn't ask Yahweh to bring a potter. I should never have left it to fate."

Ruth and Orpah exchanged a glance as eloquent as Naomi's shrug. As if a god would care, their look said, what happens to women, even if they are facing starvation.

7

HER DREAMS had been confused and chaotic so that Ruth was grateful to grope her way out of them into the serenity of early morning. She always woke early, and Mahlon had accused her once of waking him by simply lying and staring at him. She had denied it, laughing, even when she had known it was true. She had liked the defenseless, little-boy look on his face when he was sleeping, and she had enjoyed watching him when she first woke up.

But Mahlon was dead. She would never turn again to see his sleeping face or watch his eyes slowly open in awareness of her stare. Mahlon had been dead for two months, and she still had to remind herself each morning. It was not enough to look across the room to see Orpah and Naomi asleep on their mats, not enough to gaze around the small room and see the belongings that the other two women had brought when they moved in with her. Always there had to be more than a visual reminder. Ruth had to say the words deep inside herself. Mahlon is dead.

Quietly, so she would not disturb the others, Ruth stood and pulled on her outer garment. Knotting a cord around her waist, she slipped, bare footed, to the door and let herself out. Blinking, she stared at the day. The air moved with a chill whisper across the yard, but the sun was bright and the sky shone with brilliance. It would be a lovely day, the sort of day that came only in late winter, warm and clear, with neither rain nor heat to spoil it.

Across the yard, beyond the kiln, a small almond tree spread itself against the sky. Pale infant blossoms blurred the tips of the branches. Ruth walked toward the tree with a sense of wonder. She hadn't noticed that the buds were ready for blossoming, so the tiny flowers were a miracle.

If Mahlon were alive, I would have noticed sooner, Ruth said to herself and knew it wasn't true. She had never been able to talk to Mahlon about the things she loved or, for that matter, the things she grieved over.

Then why have I been blind to the swelling buds, Ruth wondered. It can't be just because I've been so busy helping Orpah and Naomi move and trying to help with the pottery. I've been busy before. And I've known something of grief before this, the grief of my inability to have a child. But always, until now, I've been aware of the world. What has happened to me now?

Ruth reached up and touched one small blossom. Here, in these fragile petals, was the hope of tomorrow, the promise of harvest. As though several seasons passed in front of her eyes, Ruth saw the fall of the petals, the swelling knob left on the branch, the growth and development of the oval nut with its thin shell protected by an outer covering.

But there is no hope for *me*, Ruth discovered all at once. I didn't see the buds swelling because there is no promise in *my* life. I am a widow. I live with two widows. We are empty and hopeless.

And what did you expect? It was as though Patima stood beside her, tilting an audacious face to look up into Ruth's. Did you expect happiness?

No. Ruth spoke in silence to the phantom Patima, while her hands still cupped the almond blossoms. No, I never expected happiness. And yet I must have lived with the hope of it. Now, there is not even hope.

"You're dreaming again!"

The words were so exactly what Patima would have said under the circumstances that Ruth jumped, sure that she had conjured her sister out of the morning air. But it was Orpah standing in the doorway, rubbing her eyes and peering across at her sister-in-law.

"Our mother wondered where you were, and I told her you were probably dreaming over a flower or a cloud. I wasn't wrong." Orpah's voice was amused and affectionate.

Ruth smiled at her. "I didn't want to wake you scrabbling around for my sandals, and I didn't want to walk to the well without them."

"Well, it's my turn to go to the well anyhow," Orpah returned. "Come and get your sandals; the ground is still cold. We'll eat first and then I'll go for water."

"Have you seen the almond tree?" Ruth asked, walking back toward the house. "Have you noticed that it's blooming?"

"I was looking at it yesterday," Orpah said. "It's young, but it has a nice show of blossom. There ought to be a decent crop of nuts before next winter."

"It's beautiful," Ruth said.

"I suppose so," Orpah answered. "I was thinking only of the almonds we would have."

As I should have been, Ruth realized.

Naomi's voice came from inside the house. "Ruth. Orpah. The food is ready. Come, and we'll eat."

The three women sat on the floor, facing each other across a mat of woven cloth.

"Since Mahlon died," Naomi said abruptly, "I haven't been able to pray, to ask Yahweh to bless us. But today, I'll try."

The younger woman waited obediently, their hands passive in their laps.

Naomi lifted her head and closed her eyes. "Yahweh, my Lord," she intoned and stopped. When she spoke again, her voice was thin and bitter. "Why do you curse me, my

God? Why do you heap your anger upon my head? Why do you fill my life and my daughters' lives with bitterness? What have I done?"

She opened her eyes and stared at Ruth and Orpah. "Perhaps it's because I left Bethlehem, left my own land and came to the land of strangers."

"I didn't leave *my* land," Orpah protested. "Why am *I* being punished?"

But Ruth only looked at her mother-in-law. "Strangers?" she asked softly. "Am I still a stranger, Mother?"

A look of shame touched Naomi's face. "Not you," she muttered. "Of course not you. Neither of you."

"But the others?" Ruth persisted. "My sister, Patima, our neighbors, my parents?"

Naomi's lips tightened. "Yes," she snapped. "To me they're strangers. All of them. How could you possibly understand when you've never been in a foreign land?"

"But you came because you were hungry," Ruth insisted. "Or nearly so. And we welcomed you, didn't we?"

"Do you think of Israelites as you do of your own people?" Naomi argued.

Ruth shook her head slowly. "No, I guess not. But you, Mother, and my lord, Mahlon —"

The words faded into silence and for a little while, no one said anything.

Orpah spoke abruptly. "You didn't ask for your god's blessing. You only asked why he had punished you. Should we wait for you to ask a blessing on us?" Her eyes touched the wheat cakes and olives and cheese on the mat in front of them and then lifted to Naomi's.

Unexpectedly, Naomi relaxed. "I think so much about pain," she admitted, "that I forget about the possibility of blessing." She closed her eyes again. "Pour your blessing on us, O Yahweh. Even on this household of empty women, pour out your blessing."

For the space of several heart beats, there was silence, but it was a comfortable sort of silence. Ruth felt an odd loosening of the restriction that had bound her ever since Mahlon's death.

With a courage she had never dreamed she'd have, she spoke of the thing that had tormented her ever since Mahlon had fallen. "It's my fault." Her voice was clear and precise. "I'm the one who's being punished, Mother, and you have to suffer because of it."

"Your fault?" Naomi looked astonished. "What did you do?"

"I was jealous." Ruth glanced at Orpah before she dropped her eyes. "I was jealous of Orpah. I wasn't willing to share my lord with her. If I had been obedient, the accident might never have happened. I was gone a long time that morning, don't you remember? I was talking to Patima about Orpah and my lord."

There was another silence, extended this time. Orpah kept her eyes on the floor, but Naomi stared at Ruth unwaveringly. Ruth met the steady look with courage in spite of the fear that pounded through her body. It had seemed right in that brief, peaceful aftermath of Naomi's prayer to make her confession, to share the terrible guilt that filled her dreams and her days. But perhaps she had been wrong. Perhaps she had given Naomi a cause for more pain and even estrangement.

When Naomi finally spoke, the words were not at all what Ruth expected. "And why," Naomi asked slowly, "would Yahweh punish you when you don't acknowledge Him as your God?"

"I don't pray to Chemosh at all," Ruth admitted.

"But do you pray to Yahweh?"

"He wouldn't listen to me," Ruth cried. "He knows I'm evil and jealous."

Almost miraculously, it seemed to Ruth, Naomi's face softened. "Do you realize what you're saying, my child?" she whispered. "You're saying that Yahweh has looked into your heart. Would He care about you if you didn't believe?"

Orpah interrupted, her face pink with embarrassment. "May I eat, Mother? If I don't get to the well soon, Ishbal will be arriving at the pottery and there won't be any water for him to work with."

"Of course, my dear. Forgive me. Here, help yourself. Ruth, you, too. We'll talk later."

Orpah heaped food in her bowl, and in a few seconds the others followed her example. But the food seemed to stick in Ruth's throat, so that she had to wash down each bite with swallows of water.

Naomi watched Ruth for a minute and then deliberately turned her attention away. "Speaking of Ishbal," she said carelessly, "I thought at first that we were indeed lucky to find a man who claimed he knew the pottery trade and who was willing to take Chilion's house for salary. Now I'm not so sure."

Ruth swallowed the olive she had been chewing and answered. "He has none of the skill of my lord Mahlon. Or Chilion either. His jars and bowls are thick and coarse; his water pots are awkward. My lord's hands were almost magic in their skill. Ishbal has none of that."

"And Chilion used the slip so beautifully," Orpah added. "The pottery was pretty as well as practical when —"

"When the sons of Elimelech made it," Naomi finished. "I know. I've been wanting to talk about it."

Orpah wiped the back of her hand across her mouth. "I'll let you and my sister decide if anything can be done," she said. "I must hurry to the well."

"You're right," Naomi approved. "You'll probably have to make several trips to the well today. Or maybe Ruth or I can go once or twice. Ishbal is so careless with the water that we need a lot of it."

"It's going to be such a nice day," Orpah said, "that going to the well might be almost pleasant — if we could carry empty jars both ways, that is."

Her smile was rueful, and Naomi and Ruth smiled in

sympathy. But when Orpah had left the room, Naomi turned toward Ruth and her smile faded.

"What do you really think about Ishbal, Ruth? Can he handle the business or ought we try to find another potter?"

Ruth gave up any attempt to eat and began to gather together the bowls and food. "He's a dreadful potter," she said, emptying olives into a tall jar. "But he's the only one in the village. When Ishbal came from Edom (I'm beginning to think now that he ran away from some potter he'd been apprenticed to), like you, I thought we were lucky. But no one wants to buy his pots. Orpah does all the treading and I've been doing all the wedging, so the clay is well prepared. It's just —"

"He has no skill," Naomi said. "It's as you said before, he has no skill. So what shall we do?"

"What can we do? You know none of us can make pots."

Naomi nodded. "When Elimelech and I were young, I used to think it looked easy. Until he let me try it one day."

"Well, you saw what happened when I tried right after Mahlon died."

The two women smiled sympathetically at one another.

Ruth's face sobered. "Mother, can you forgive me for what I confessed? Can you still care for me when I've admitted that I was disobedient and jealous? It really might be my fault that Mahlon died."

Naomi's smile also faded. "It would be easy," she admitted. "It would be easy to blame you so I could ease my own pain. But how do I know if you're right? Tell me, my child, how did you feel about your decision after you had talked to Patima? What were you going to tell Mahlon?"

"I was going to say it was all right. Truly I was, Mother. I knew that what Patima had told me was right — that if I refused I would gain nothing except your anger. Yours and my lord's. I knew I couldn't have endured that. Better by far to share my lord than to lose my place in his house, and my place in your heart."

"So then," Naomi said in a very matter-of-fact tone, "Can you be blamed? Did you feel bitterness toward me or my son?"

"I was unhappy," Ruth said. "Or I should say I was angry."

After a moment Naomi spoke. "But I really can't blame you. You behaved as any girl might — any girl who was not an Israelite?"

"Mother," Ruth began, but Naomi interrupted.

"An Israelite would have understood the law," she said. "I suppose even then she could have been jealous, but she wouldn't have been so shocked."

Naomi's understanding warmed Ruth. "Thank you," she said.

"Sometimes," Naomi said, "sometimes I think I ought to go home. Back to Bethlehem."

"It's a long way," Ruth protested, hardly realizing what she was saying. "We'd have to go with some sort of caravan. It wouldn't be safe for women if we didn't."

Naomi stared at her in astonishment. "You mean you'd go with me?"

"You're the mother of my husband," Ruth said simply. "And, besides —" But she could not say what she was feeling.

She suddenly thought of Patima. Could she possibly leave Patima and Patima's children?

"Don't talk about going away," Ruth begged. "We'll work it out, Mother. Somehow we will."

There was a sudden crash from the pottery, and a man's voice roared through the morning. "I need water. Look, you've dropped that jar and smashed it. Now, go for more water. At once."

Naomi and Ruth hurried to the door and were in time to see Orpah hurrying out of the pottery, a jar clutched in her arms, tears running down her face.

She fled across the yard to Naomi. "He said something

indecent to me," she choked out. "And when I tried to move away, the jar dropped. I'm sorry, Mother."

Naomi's face hardened. "Take the two extra jars off the shelf, Ruth," she snapped, "and then both of you go for more water. I'll take care of Ishbal."

8

NAOMI HURRIED across the yard toward the pottery, and for a few seconds, Orpah and Ruth stood watching her. When they turned to each other, a stricken look etched both faces.

"Did he touch you?" Ruth asked. "Did he hurt you?"

Orpah swallowed and tried to speak calmly. "No, not really. He grabbed for me; that's why the jar got smashed. He's — he's revolting."

"Try not to think about it. I know Mother will take care of him." The sound of voices, raised in anger, came to them. "In fact," Ruth added, risking a small smile, "I could almost find it in me to feel sorry for Ishbal."

But Orpah shook her head. "He's cruel. You didn't see his face. I wish it were a man facing up to him."

The sound of a slap cracked suddenly, followed by total silence. Without a word, Ruth set her jar on the ground and flew across the yard, Orpah close behind. Breathless, they reached the door of the pottery and looked in to see Naomi staring at Ishbal with her hand cupped against her face.

"Mother!" Ruth exclaimed. "Did he hit you? Mother, answer me."

But Naomi seemed unable to speak and her eyes were fastened with horrified fascination on the face of the man in front of her.

"Did you hit her?" Ruth turned to Ishbal in fury.

His voice was sullen. "No woman can tell me what to do or what not to do."

"She's the owner of this pottery. You work for her," Ruth cried.

"And who would believe her word over mine?" Ishbal sneered. "She's a foreigner. Even if she weren't, what man in the village would believe that she had the right to yell at me? I'm not a Moabite, but I'm a man, and people would believe me, not her."

"I'll speak to my father," Ruth began but Ishbal interrupted.

"I've already spoken to your father about the possibility of marrying you when your mourning period is over. He'll be glad to have you taken off his hands, so why would he cause trouble for me?"

Ruth stared at the man with revulsion crawling in her. She had hardly heard what he said after the shocking words "the possibility of marrying you."

"You spoke to my father about marriage?" she asked in a strained voice.

The man's expression was smug. "Not every man would take a widow. But a widow with a pottery — ah, there's the difference."

Naomi's voice was thick with anger. "My daughters-in-law are not part of the price of the business."

"I'll slap you again," Ishbal threatened, moving toward Naomi, his hand lifted.

Ruth deliberately placed herself between the man and her mother-in-law. She was, she discovered gratefully, taller than Ishbal. Perhaps he hadn't realized that yet. She made it as obvious as possible by pulling herself very straight and standing close to him so that he had to look up into her face.

"I don't belong to my father anymore," she stated, "and he can't dispose of me so lightly. I belong to my mother-in-law and to her husband's family. If you touch her again, I'll call on my brother-in-law who will be more sympathetic toward me than my father. He'll flatten your ambitions and you, as a man flattens a bug."

Ishbal's arrogance faltered before her scorn, and he dropped the lifted hand. "I don't plan to hit her again. But a man doesn't have to put up with bossiness."

"You call it bossiness to protect my daughter-in-law from your indecent advances?" Naomi said, her voice sharp.

Before Ishbal could answer, Ruth spoke suddenly. "And if you've been thinking of marrying me, why is it that you made improper advances to my sister?"

Ishbal's smile was oily. "Perhaps I can have two wives. If it was suitable for the Israelite, why not for me?"

The three women stared at him. How could he possibly have known that, Ruth wondered. Patima would never have repeated it. She glanced at Orpah and saw the misery in her face. Of course. Orpah could have confided in one of her sisters or a cousin who, in turn, could have told a husband. And men were prone to gossip. Every wife knew that men talked about more than the law or business when they sat together in the market place. So it was possible for Ishbal to know.

"You're loathesome," Ruth spit out.

"I didn't think *you'd* be offended," Ishbal whined, suddenly humble. "Most young women hate their mothers-in-law even though they don't dare show it."

"Well, I don't hate mine." Ruth's voice was cold. "And unless you want to have to do all the treading and wedging yourself, as well as turning the pots, you'd better treat all of us with respect. I swear to you that I will go to my sister's husband who's the head man in this village, as you well know. Remember, I'm not an Israelite. I have some influence."

Ishbal nodded eagerly. "I know. I was irritated this morning, and the small one — she made me mad. It won't happen again."

Ruth looked down at his ingratiating smile with disdain.

Then she turned on her heel and walked away, followed by Naomi and Orpah.

The man was insufferable, Ruth raged inside her mind. But in spite of her contempt, fear coiled inside her stomach. Ishbal might have been ingratiating, there at the end of the conversation, but he was insolent and arrogant and what was more, he was right. As a man, he would have the sympathy of nearly every other man in the village. Even Faran would be reluctant to speak in behalf of a woman.

Oh, Mahlon, Ruth thought with despair, we need you now.

They had almost reached the door of the house when Ishbal shouted out with a brave, new show of confidence. "I need water. Bring it to me immediately."

Naomi hurried past Ruth to pick up the water jars from the ground. Thrusting them into Ruth's and Orpah's hands, she spoke wearily. "Let's get the water. Wait — I'll get another jar, and we'll all three go so he should be well supplied. And from this time on, none of us will enter the pottery alone when that man is there. Now, come, let's hurry!"

They made the trip to and from the well in silence. Several times it seemed to Ruth that Naomi was getting ready to speak, but each time she apparently swallowed the words. Ruth and Orpah were silent, too. There was so much that clamored to be said, but none of them seemed to know how to begin.

Twice they walked to the well and twice they carried their heavy water jars back to the pottery. They emptied the water into the waiting bowls and pots, each woman avoiding Ishbal's eyes and walking away in silence.

The potter spoke as they were leaving the second time. "I need someone to wedge some clay," he barked. "How do you expect me to make decent pots if I have to waste time preparing the clay?"

Ruth longed to say that no one would expect him to make decent pots because it was obvious that he didn't know how. But, with an effort, she held back the words. Nothing would be gained in angering the man further.

"I'll wedge the clay," she said. "My sister-in-law and mother-in-law will do some treading if it needs to be done."

"Of course it needs to be done," Ishbal snarled. "You've been running back and forth to the well all morning, just because that stupid woman dropped and smashed a water pot. I'd suggest you all get busy."

Ruth did not bother answering him, and Naomi and Orpah started toward the door.

"We'll be only a few feet away," Naomi said with a warning look at Ishbal. His face flushed with anger, but he said nothing as Naomi walked out, holding Orpah's arm as she went.

Ruth lifted some wet clay onto the table and began the stiff, rhythmic kneading that made the clay suitable for use. Several times she was aware that Ishbal was watching her but she ignored him. Finally, when the clay was properly wedged, she stopped and flexed her shoulders.

"You work well," Ishbal said.

Ruth met his eyes. "My husband was a good teacher," she answered.

Before Ishbal could speak again, she turned away. "We'll return after our midday meal," she announced. She remembered that Naomi had offered to share their food with him the first few days he had worked at the pottery. She knew that would never happen again.

Without waiting for an answer, she hurried to the yard, calling to Naomi. "I'll fix the food, Mother. You and Orpah come as soon as you can."

Naomi nodded in assent, and Ruth crossed the yard to her house. While her hands put cheese and olives and bread out on the coarse mat she had spread in the middle of the floor, her mind darted in a dozen different directions.

What were they going to do? Ishbal had created an impossible situation. He was in a position to hurt them all, and there was little they could do in retaliation. Oh, Naomi could try to force him to leave, but then what? A pottery without a potter — even an inefficient potter — was nothing. What would they live on? There were no longer good pots to trade for food.

Naomi and Orpah, stopping long enough to rinse their feet in the basin that stood outside the door, came in, and Ruth looked up to see in their faces the same strain and worry that she knew must be evident on her own.

"We'll eat," Naomi announced. "After I've prayed, we'll eat. And then we'll talk. We have much to talk about, my daughters."

In spite of her attempt at confidence, her voice broke badly on the final words. Avoiding each other's eyes, the women sat on the floor and waited for Naomi to address her god.

"Yahweh, my Lord," Naomi intoned. "I am only a woman. These daughters of mine are only women. But we need your guidance and help. We are lost. Bless us and keep us. Amen."

It was a simple prayer, Ruth thought, remembering the breast beating and chanting of the priests of Chemosh. Since there was no incense, no priests, no ceremony, she couldn't believe that the prayer would have any effect. Well, it might comfort Naomi a little. Even that would be something.

When the small meal had been eaten and cleared away, Naomi asked the younger women to sit down again.

"We're in trouble," she confided softly. "I think in greater trouble than I have realized. Ishbal is not only incompetent, he's evil. Perhaps I shouldn't be so blunt," she added hastily to Ruth, "since he has spoken to your father about marriage."

Ruth's face was solemn. "My father no longer owns me. If you don't relinquish your claim on me, I'm not — I'm not available to Ishbal."

"Nor I," Orpah said quickly, her eyes shadowed with memories of the morning.

"I will never relinquish my claims on you," Naomi vowed. "Not until you ask me to — or until I think it's best for you. As far as I'm concerned, as far as our law is concerned, you still belong to the house of Elimelech."

"But if Ishbal is persistent?" Orpah ventured.

"He won't be persistent when he learns that he can have the pottery without the obligation of taking one of the women," Naomi said.

"You mean you'll sell it to him outright?" Ruth cried.

Naomi hesitated for a minute, her head bowed. "If I can find a way to get to Bethlehem," she said at last, "then I'll leave this place and go back to the home of my fathers."

She shook her head when an automatic sound of protest came from the younger women. "I'm sure Patima will provide a home for you, Ruth, and, Orpah, your mother has already admitted to me that she and your father are getting old. With no sons to keep them, they would welcome a daughter who could stay with them and take care of them in their old age."

"But, Mother," Orpah began.

"I've been thinking all morning," Naomi interrupted. "It's the only thing to do. If you don't have any responsibility toward me, you'll be free. And if Ishbal can buy the pottery outright, he'll lose interest in marriage."

Naomi looked at Ruth and smiled. "Not, my dear," she said, "that I don't think you're worthy of marriage, but after Mahlon, I don't think you want Ishbal."

"After Mahlon," Ruth murmured, her voice catching, "I don't want anyone."

"Your grief is fresh," Naomi said. "But you're young and you will heal. Perhaps some day, Patima's lord will find a man who will be good to you."

Ruth stood up. "I don't want to talk about it anymore," she said with conviction. "It's too sudden, all of this. Maybe we can work something out so you won't have to leave, Mother."

"No," Naomi insisted. "I want to leave. I'm homesick for

my family and my friends. I'm sure I have sisters living. And I feel a need to go back to the land where Yahweh reigns."

"Even if it means leaving us?" Orpah whispered.

"Leaving you will break my heart," Naomi admitted. "But I just don't know what else to do."

Orpah leaned over and kissed Naomi's cheek. "Ruth's right," she murmured. "Let's not talk about it now. Maybe something will turn up."

"And besides," Ruth said harshly, "your heart doesn't have to be broken. Not on my account at least. I'll go with you."

Naomi looked up to where Ruth was striding agitatedly back and forth across the room. "Your duty touches me, Ruth. Truly it does. But —"

"And you're not being practical," Ruth insisted, hardly aware that she was interrupting her mother-in-law. "How would we get there? We've talked about it before. We'd need a caravan — not just any caravan but a decent one, made up of good, decent men. Men who wouldn't hurt defenseless widows. Where would we ever find anything like that?"

"If the caravans that go through here," Orpah added, "are any example, I don't think there *is* such a thing as a decent one. The men are always a rough and ragged lot. They look like men who did nothing but kick their donkeys — and probably their women."

Naomi sat very still. When she spoke, her voice was hushed. "I'll ask Yahweh," she announced. "I'll ask Him to provide the right kind of caravan. If I'm to go home, if it's right that I make these plans, then He'll take care of me. He parted the sea for the Israelites fleeing Egypt. Surely He can bring a caravan of honest men through Bezer."

"On their way to Bethlehem?" Ruth asked and knew that her skepticism was obvious in her voice.

"On their way to Bethlehem." Naomi's words were firm.

Ruth stared at her mother-in-law while a small crinkle of

chill moved across the back of her neck. As bitter as Naomi was over the loss of her husband and sons, she still displayed a faith different from any Ruth had ever known.

"Mother," Ruth said slowly, "if your god provides such a miracle as that — if he sends a caravan of decent men through here who will take us to Bethlehem, I'll — I'll not only go with you, I'll know that your god is a mighty god. The true God."

Naomi's eyes shone. "All the more reason for my prayers to be answered," she said. The confidence in her voice made a warm, steady sound in the small room.

9

"EVEN IF A CARAVAN of that type came through Bezer, you can't go to Bethlehem with Naomi." Patima, her fists planted on her hips, glared up at Ruth with a mixture of dismay and anger. "What would I do?"

Ruth smiled. "You have your husband, our parents, your children, and all the other folks of Bezer. You don't need me."

"I need you," Patima argued. "You're my sister."

"I know. Leaving you will be the most terrible part of all. But, Patima, Naomi needs me more than you do. I belong to her and to her husband's family. You know the law."

Patima was not convinced. "She wouldn't hold you to it. You know she wouldn't. I can understand your feeling of loyalty to her, and if she stayed here in Bezer, I'd never expect you to be other than faithful to her. But to go to Bethlehem..."

Ruth tried to laugh, but her voice shook. "You make it sound as though I were going into the regions of everlasting darkness."

"Don't joke!" Patima's voice was fierce. "We'd never see each other again."

"I know."

"Listen." Patima's voice was wheedling. "My husband was saying only the other day that we were going to have to

77

find someone to come in and stay with us to help with the children. We were thinking of his father's sister. But I'd much rather have you. The children already love you more than anyone else. Wouldn't that be an answer?"

Ruth stood looking at Patima, wishing fervently that these coaxing words had never been spoken. Choosing to go with Naomi was not so hard when the only alternative had been life with Ishbal or a lonely life shared with no one. Now, there was the possibility of a life that would hold love and fulfillment.

"You shouldn't have said that," Ruth whispered.

"Why not? I know, from my own conversations with her, that Naomi wouldn't blame you if you stayed. Oh, Ruth, don't go away." Patima's usually merry face was drawn and pleading.

Ruth shook herself mentally. "Why are we acting like this?" she said, trying to make her voice light. "Why are we acting as though my going were assured? I can't go unless a caravan comes through. And not just any old caravan, but one made up of good men *and* going to Bethlehem. Can you even imagine that happening?"

"But you say Naomi has been praying about it?"

"Well, yes, but what's that? No priest, no sacrifice, no incense to burn. What would a woman's words mean to Yahweh, to any god?" But even as she spoke, Ruth was remembering Naomi's conviction — and her faith.

Patima must have seen the uncertainty reflected in Ruth's eyes. "But you're not entirely sure her prayers *won't* be answered, are you?"

Ruth shook her head. "I'll tell you what I told her. I said that if such a caravan came through, I'd not only go with her gladly, I'd believe her god was truly a mighty god."

"Did you mean it?"

"Of course I meant it. Can you even conceive what it would be like to know a god heard the simple prayers of a *woman*? How could I help believing?"

Patima stared at her for a few seconds and then smiled.

"Well, I don't know why I'm worrying about it. Such a caravan won't come through here, and so I'm going to forget it. But if Naomi gets so desperate to go back to Bethlehem that she tries to find another way to leave, don't forget that you're welcome in my house. In my lord's house," she added.

"You know I'm grateful," Ruth mumbled, worrying that her words might sound stiff and unfeeling. "You know — well, you must know that I love you."

The last three words came out with a wrench that was almost painful. Women did not usually express their love except perhaps to a husband who encouraged such lavishness of praise. Mahlon never had, and so the words were stilted and awkward on Ruth's tongue.

Patima merely smiled, reached up to kiss Ruth's cheek and then bent for her water jar and turned to start home. But just before she left, she looked back at her sister. "You know I feel the same," she said and hurried away.

Ruth shouldered her jar of water and started slowly for the pottery. Her thoughts were in chaos. She believed with all her heart that her place was with Naomi, that her responsibility was to care for Mahlon's mother. But with Patima's invitation glowing in her mind, the way of duty seemed more difficult than she had ever dreamed it would be.

Oh, well, she thought, Patima's right. The caravan will never come and I'm stupid to worry. I'll still be living in Bezer, caring for Naomi or for Patima's children, even when I'm old.

The days trudged past. Ishbal was never as cruel or lecherous as he had been the day he slapped Naomi, but the relationship between him and the women was strained. They distrusted and feared him, and he took advantage of their timidity.

Every day the strain intensified. Ruth watched Naomi's desperation grow. It seemed as though the longer she lived without husband and sons, the more she suffered. There was apparently no healing for her anywhere. Evidently the difficulties with Ishbal consumed her, so that if she had ever known contentment or peace in the land of Moab, she had forgotten it now. All she talked about was the possibility of going home. Her prayers were filled with a pleading for a caravan to come.

And one day it came.

Ruth and Orpah were both at the well. They had left Naomi at home to grind the grain for bread, and they had walked slowly through the spring morning, dreading the walk back with the heavy jars.

"If women only had to walk *to* the well," Orpah said lightly, "life would be much easier. It's the weight of the water that makes things hard."

"We'd all get fat and lazy if we had only empty jars to carry," Ruth responded.

"I wouldn't mind having a chance to find out," Orpah said, and they laughed together.

They turned the last corner and there, not far from the well, they saw the gathering of men and donkeys. Several of the women were drawing water for the men, and that, itself, was unusual, since women never paid attention to strangers. Unless the men had demanded it, of course. Perhaps that was what happened.

But when Ruth and Orpah got closer, they saw that the men were staying decorously away from the women, and it was a strange woman, hardly more than a girl, who stood by the well and gratefully accepted the jars of water and carried them to the men.

The girl was returning to the well when Ruth reached it. The stranger smiled shyly.

"Peace," she said in a soft, breathless voice. "May Yahweh grant you peace."

Ruth stopped as though she had been struck. She stared at the girl, her mouth dry.

"Have I offended you?" the girl asked anxiously. "I meant no harm. My name is Altah, and my husband's caravan is traveling north into Israel. Did I do wrong to speak of my God here?"

It was Orpah who found the words to answer. "Forgive my sister," she said. "She is struck dumb by the shock of your words. You see — you see, she and I were married to Israelites, to men who called on Yahweh."

Altah's face lighted. "Truly? Then I feel as though I have met friends."

Ruth wet her lips with the tip of her tongue. "I bid you welcome," she said with an effort. "Your husband's caravan is heading for Israel, you said?"

Altah nodded. "We've been in Moab for about ten years, but now we've heard that the fields around Bethlehem are green again, that there will be a rich harvest in another month. So we're going home." Her face blazed with excitement. "I was just a child when my parents and some others (my husband's parents among them) came to Moab. But, even so, I remember the home of my fathers, and I can't wait to get back."

The girl was talking so eagerly that at first she didn't seem to notice Ruth's lack of response. Then, looking more closely, she said, "What is it? You look so pale. Are you ill?" She glanced at Orpah for assistance.

Orpah took Ruth's arm. "Here, my sister. Sit here on this stone. You look terrible."

Ruth sat on the low rock and, after carefully setting her jar beside her, slowly lifted her head so that she was looking into the face of the young stranger.

"You did say Bethlehem, didn't you?" Ruth asked, her voice cracking with the strain.

"Yes. Do you know of it? Is it possible that your husband is from that area?"

"My husband is dead," Ruth said.

"Oh, I'm sorry." The girl flushed with embarrassment.

"Our husbands are both dead," Orpah offered. "And our father-in-law also. His name was Elimilech. Our mother-in-law, Naomi, is still with us, but that's all."

"And she wants to —" Ruth began but Orpah shook her head.

"Wait," Orpah cautioned. "Strangers won't be interested in what our mother-in-law wants."

Ruth understood at once. Orpah was hoping that Naomi could be kept from hearing of this caravan —

"No, Orpah, you're wrong," Ruth said. "Mother will have to know. If Yahweh has sent this caravan, then —"

"You believe in our God?" Altah said in a wondering voice. "And you think He sent us through here?"

Ruth patted the ground with invitation and after a quick glance toward the caravan, Altah dropped down beside her.

"My mother-in-law longs to go home," Ruth explained. "She's had many troubles here. So she's been praying that Yahweh would send a caravan. She prayed for a caravan of decent people going to Bethlehem. Can anyone possibly doubt that her prayers have now been answered?"

Altah was round-eyed at Ruth's disclosure, but before she could say anything, Orpah spoke vehemently. "We can't be ready to go in a day. Or even two. And surely these people won't be able to wait for us. So even though the caravan has come, that doesn't mean that we must travel on with it. Or even that they'd permit us to go with them."

But Altah spoke up quickly. "We had planned to ask permission to pitch our tents in this vicinity for a few days — if we could have access to the well, that is. Two of the men are ill or hurt. One has a fever of some kind and another stepped in a hole yesterday and twisted his ankle. We need to rest a few days. We're not in any particular rush to get to Bethlehem. As long as we get there in time for the barley harvest, it will be all right."

Ruth felt a stabbing of grief but at the same time, she was aware of awe and reverence in her. The pain, she knew, came from her certainty that she would be leaving Bezer, leaving Patima and Patima's children, leaving her parents, her friends, and a lifetime of memories. But the grief could not extinguish the strange reverence that spread through her like the warmth of a fire on a cold winter night.

The coming of the caravan, a family caravan of people who worshiped Yahweh, and the fact that it was heading for Bethlehem could not be understood in any other light than as a direct answer to prayer. Naomi had prayed with no other authority than that of her faith, and her God had heard her. He must have a reason for hearing, Ruth thought, a reason greater than simply providing for an aging widow to get back to her people. But that didn't change the fact that He heard and He answered, practically speaking, an impossible request.

"Do you think," Ruth said to Altah, "that your husband and his family would let us travel with you? I'm sure my mother-in-law will have enough silver after we sell the pottery to pay our way — and enough to buy a donkey for her to ride as well."

"Let me ask him," Altah said, getting to her feet. "I'll tell him about the prayer," she flung over her shoulder.

"You still don't have to tell her," Orpah pleaded. "We can still keep it a secret."

"You're mad," Ruth said curtly. "If they stay here near the village for several days, she couldn't help but hear about them. Besides, why would we hide a miracle?"

"I don't want a miracle," Orpah wailed. "I don't want to go to some strange place where I won't know anyone."

"You don't have to go, Ruth said, somehow keeping her voice warm and reassuring. "Mother has already said you can stay with your own parents. You don't have to go."

"But you're going."

"Well, of course. I promised I would. I said that if a caravan came —"

"I talked to Patima," Orpah interrupted. "I know she has asked you to live with them. How can you refuse her?"

"You think it's easy?" Ruth asked slowly. "But, no, you know it's not easy. Only, can't you see? It's so plain that Yahweh wants us to go."

"Naomi's god wants *her* to go," Orpah insisted. "It doesn't have anything to do with us."

"Has Chemosh ever answered your prayers like that?" Ruth countered. "Giving you what you begged for without needing a priest to intercede? Has he?"

"Yahweh didn't answer her prayers when she begged for Chilion not to die." Orpah's voice was sullen.

Ruth hesitated. "I can't begin to understand that. I only know that I promised if a caravan came — a particular caravan — I would believe. And I do," she finished simply.

"Oh, Ruth," Orpah cried. "I just don't think I can bear it."

At that moment, Altah came hurrying over to them. "My lord says yes," she said. "He says there's always room for our own people. He thinks he might remember your father-in-law, Elimelech. Did they come to Moab more than ten years ago?"

Ruth nodded, and Altah laughed with satisfaction. "Then your mother-in-law is almost a distant relative of mine. I have an uncle on my mother's side — Boaz — who is related to your father-in-law. Well, he isn't really my uncle, but his wife was my mother's sister. She's dead now, but I still think of him as an uncle."

Ruth smiled, touched by the girl's enthusiasm. "Then I shall think of you as my cousin," she said softly. "And will you tell your lord that we're grateful for his words of welcome? Now, if you'll excuse me, I'll run to tell my mother-in-law the news. Later, when she's over the shock and the surprise, I'll bring you to meet her. Just now, I must talk to her alone."

"Of course," Altah said. "We'll pitch our tents on the north side of town, my husband says. The men of the village have already given their permission. I'll look for you soon."

In her excitement, Ruth hurried off without her jar of

water, but Orpah called her back. Ruth, looking into Orpah's saddened face, felt a quick rush of compassion.

"Come, my sister," she said gently. "We'll go and tell our mother of this miraculous thing. And in her joy, who knows, she may relinquish all claim on you so that you can stay here without any regret or shame."

"Truly?"

"Truly," Ruth said. "Now let's hurry. I can hardly wait to see her face."

part II

But Ruth said, "Do not urge me to leave you or turn back from following you; for where you go, I will go, and where you lodge, I will lodge. Your people shall be my people, and your God, my God."... So they both went until they came to Bethlehem.   Ruth 1:16, 19*a*

10

DAWN ENTERED THE SMALL ROOM with a hesitant light. Ruth, who had been awake for a long time, lay without moving and stared about the room as the growing light picked out details that had been obscured by the dark.

I'll never see it again, Ruth thought. I'll never be sheltered from the rain by this roof or these walls. I'll never sit on this floor to eat or spin or grind grain. After today, this house will be only a memory for me.

The memories of the past four days filled her. It didn't seem possible that only four days could hold so much joy and pain and work. Ruth let the memories flow through her mind like beads slipping through her fingers. Naomi's joy, Patima's pain, Orpah's uncertainty, Ishbal's covetousness all formed a shifting mosaic of moments to be remembered.

She would never forget the way Naomi's face had lit up when she had heard of the caravan. Her eyes had shone with awe, and although she hadn't said much, it was obvious that she believed a miracle had been granted them.

Patima's pain had been as intense as Naomi's joy. At first Patima had argued and cajoled and begged, and then she had said simply, "So you'll go. I guess I knew you would. You couldn't do anything different and still be you. But it will be like a death for me. I don't think I can bear it."

"I'm not sure I can bear it either," Ruth had confessed, and they had stood staring at each other, too stricken for tears.

The memories slid faster through Ruth's mind. She tried to blot out the recollection of Ishbal's greed and of her father's indifference.

Well, she told herself, all men are alike, in a way. They are trained from infancy to think only of themselves. Even Mahlon, as good as he was, lived primarily for Mahlon. Perhaps this was one reason she was willing to go with Naomi. There might be more kindness in a house where a woman made the decisions.

"How long have you been awake, Ruth?" Naomi's voice was so clear that Ruth knew she, too, had been unable to sleep.

"For a long time," Ruth said. "And we must get up. The caravan will be starting shortly after sunrise."

"Yes, I know. Orpah, are you awake?"

Orpah's voice was muffled. "Yes, Mother."

It was obvious that she had been weeping. Ruth felt mingled pity and irritation touch her. Orpah had no desire to go to Bethlehem and she obviously felt no awe at Yahweh's miracle. If she thought of it at all, she must have considered the arrival of the caravan as a shocking coincidence that had disrupted her life.

But she was stubborn. No matter how many times Naomi assured Orpah that she could stay in Bezer, she only answered that if Ruth was going, she would go.

It's foolish, Ruth thought, tying the thongs of her leather sandals around her ankles. If I were thinking only of Naomi, I'd never move a step out of this town.

The thought was totally unexpected. She sat quietly, staring at her foot in its sandal. But of course she was thinking of Naomi, wasn't she? Why else would she be tearing out the roots of her life so that at times she thought she could not stand the pain of it?

It's because of Yahweh, she realized with a slow sense of

wonder. I care about Naomi; of course I do. And I know that Mahlon's death doesn't take away my duty toward her. But it's more than Naomi. It's Naomi's God. This is what Orpah doesn't feel and will never be able to understand.

"Orpah," Naomi said sternly. "You're crying again. I want something settled right now before we join the caravan, before you have done something you'll regret all your life."

"Yes, Mother?" Orpah's voice sounded as swollen as her eyes were.

"I want you to stay here. Not in this house, of course. It now belongs to Ishbal. But here in this town. Before we get away from the security of Bezer, I want you to reconsider."

Orpah stared at Naomi, and Ruth sat without moving. In a sense, they had made their start toward Bethlehem last night when they had carried their last bundles to where the caravan waited, north of town.

"Both of you," Naomi said firmly. "Ruth, you haven't cried as much as Orpah has, but I've seen how you look when Patima or her children come by. I've thought about it all night. I want you both to stay."

Orpah burst into ready tears, and even Ruth felt an unexpected ache building up in her throat so that she found it difficult to shape words.

"No," she began, and Orpah's sodden voice joined hers in protest. "No, Mother," Orpah cried, "we'll go with you to your own country."

Naomi's voice was strong and decisive. "I tell you no! It's not that I don't love you. It's that I can't do for you what should be done."

She stopped, looking at the floor, and when she spoke again, the words poured out in a flood of bitterness. "I'm too old to marry again, so what can you hope for from me? Even if I were to marry tonight, could I bear sons for you to marry? Could I do for both of you what I tried to do once for you, Orpah?"

Ruth was silent, but she knew her face must bear the

same look of misery as Orpah's. Did Naomi think they wanted to stay with her only because she might provide a husband?

"Mother," Orpah began. "You know we don't expect you to ever have a son for us to marry."

Her voice drifted into silence, and Ruth realized that Orpah wasn't being wholly honest. Oh, of course they knew that Naomi would never marry again, never bear a son. But Orpah had been thinking of other kinsmen. Orpah had been hoping for marriage to someone in the tribe of Elimelech.

Naomi's look toward Orpah was both fond and shrewd. "I've never been a matchmaker," Naomi said softly. "You — neither of you — can look to me for a man."

Ruth spoke briskly. "That's ridiculous, Mother. You made a man for me once. I don't want another. You've been kinder than my father, more generous than any kinsman and — and more reverent than any priest of Chemosh. Let's not talk about husbands or any man at all."

Naomi came over and kissed her and then turned to Orpah and kissed her, too. "Truly, my dear," she whispered, "I won't hate you if you stay. You belong here."

Orpah cast herself into Naomi's arms and wept with mingled despair and relief. "If you truly wouldn't hate me, Mother —"

"I could never hate you. Your mother will welcome your staying. I know because I've talked to her."

"Then," Orpah began, "perhaps, if you think — if you're sure."

"I'm sure," Naomi said, her voice gentle. "I'll ask my God to bless you and care for you." She seemed to avoid looking at Ruth as she continued talking to Orpah. "Go to your mother's house now, so that I'll know for sure they can take you in today. Then come to the caravan to get your things and to say goodbye."

Orpah started for the door and then turned again to Naomi. "Mother," she began.

"Go with my blessing," Naomi said.

Orpah seemed to hang irresolutely between Naomi and the door, and then she clutched her robe around her and ran into the morning.

Naomi watched her go, and Ruth could not tell what she was feeling, so expressionless was her face. Slowly Naomi turned to Ruth.

"See," she said, "see what she has done. She has gone, and wisely, I suspect, back to her people and her gods. Won't you do the same? Won't you, my dear?"

If I were more like Orpah, Ruth thought, I'd fling my arms around her and pour out all my love and my convictions. But I'm not like Orpah. Or Patima either. I'm just myself. What can I say that will make it clear to her that it won't matter if I'm lonely or homesick or if I have regrets about leaving this place? I belong to her and to her husband's people. And, most of all, to her God.

"Mother," Ruth said at last. It wasn't until she started to talk and heard the rush of Naomi's breathing that she realized that her mother-in-law had been holding her breath, watching Ruth's face. "Mother, don't ask me to leave you. Or to stay here. Can't you understand? Wherever you go, I'll go and wherever you stay, I'll stay."

Naomi stood quietly, her eyes never leaving Ruth's.

"From now on," Ruth said, "your people will be my people and your God my God."

"You really mean it?" Naomi whispered and answered her own question. "You really mean it."

Ruth nodded. "When I die, I want to be buried where you'll be buried. Yahweh grant that nothing but death will ever separate us. Do you believe me?"

Naomi's face crumpled. "I wouldn't have held you against your will," she said.

"Then we won't talk about it anymore."

"Never," Naomi promised. She put her arms around Ruth, hugged her once and then let her go. "Now," she said, her voice so practical that no one would ever have guessed that she had just lost one daughter and kept another, "we'll eat and then we'll go."

There were more than a dozen people at the edge of town when the caravan was ready to leave. Patima, Ruth's mother and Orpah were among those who gathered to say their farewells.

Jacob, Altah's husband, was in a benevolent mood and so raised no objections to the many delays, the tears, the repeated cries of goodbye. Altah seemed to be staring with amazement at the show of love she saw.

"I hadn't known," she confided to Ruth as they started to walk away from the village, "that Moabites love as much as we do." She shot a quick look at Ruth and mumbled in apology, "Forgive me. I wasn't thinking of *you* as a Moabite."

Ruth, grateful for the talking that kept her from shedding foolish and futile tears, tried to smile. "Thank you for that. I'll be living with Israelites from now on, so life will be easier if even one person doesn't think about me as 'that Moabite.'"

Altah smiled shyly. "You wear your head scarf like an Israelite. Maybe that's it."

"It pleases my mother-in-law," Ruth admitted. "And it's not important enough to quarrel about."

"Did she wear her scarf like a Moabite while she lived in Bezer?" Altah asked.

Ruth kept her voice light. "No, not ever. But then I didn't expect her to. She's — she's a very strong woman."

"How can you bear to leave your home?" Altah blurted out. "Even though your husband is dead and you have no children, how can you stand to leave the town where you've always lived?"

Ruth searched for words. There was no easy way to tell this girl that she had made a contract with Naomi's God and He had fulfilled His part of it, so she was only doing what she had to do.

"I love my mother-in-law," she said at last. "That may seem odd but —" She spread her hands and shrugged her shoulders.

"Oh, I don't know," Altah said. "A girl who quarrels with her mother-in-law is a fool." She hesitated and then plunged on. "Most mothers are delighted to marry off their daughters to get them off their hands. And most mothers-in-law are just as glad to get daughters to help them." A faint wistfulness colored her voice. "It's not hard to like someone who needs you."

Ruth nodded. "You're young to be so wise," she said.

Altah grinned. "I'm going to have a child. So I'm old enough."

The girl had everything, Ruth thought. She was young and satisfied with her life and she was going to have a baby. Well, she was lucky then.

"My husband is beckoning to me," Altah said suddenly. "Will you be all right if I hurry on ahead? He may want me to help with one of the animals."

Not only wise but compassionate, Ruth realized suddenly. The girl had dropped back to walk with her deliberately, easing the wrench of leaving home. Perhaps she had earned her luck.

"I'm fine," Ruth insisted. "Run on ahead. If I get lonely, I'll move up to where the older women are riding. Don't worry."

Altah smiled and ran along the road until she had caught up with her husband. Ruth saw the animated exchange of conversation. Deliberately, she looked away, aware that envy was a bitter taste in her mouth.

Without really wanting to, she turned to see Bezer fading into the distance. For only a few minutes she let her eyes rest on the diminishing houses, the curve of the hill on which the pottery stood. Then, with determination, she turned her face north and did not look back again.

I've made up my mind to do what I'm doing, she thought, and to fill my mind with regret will only make things worse.

The sun was lifting into the sky and she knew the day would be hot. That's why they would travel along the top of the plateau, Jacob had told them, so that they would not have to endure the heat of the Dead Sea valley until necessary. They would travel along the edge of the hills, and when they reached the north end of the Dead Sea, they would cut down into the valley and then head west up the hills to Bethlehem.

He anticipated no more than four or five days of travel. The road was good and firm this time of year. The winter rains had nearly ended and so the danger of mud slides or sudden vicious floods sweeping down the hills was over.

Jacob had admitted when he talked to Ruth and Naomi that of course there was always the danger of outlaws. No one traveled far without thought of desert nomads and their unexpected attacks.

"But we have twenty men," Jacob had said serenely. "Twenty strong men, well armed with metal swords. And trained to protect women and supplies. I don't think you need to worry."

Well, I won't worry, Ruth told herself, stepping briskly along the dusty road. I'll leave it all in Jacob's hands.

"In Jacob's hands?" Naomi said later, when they were setting up shelters for the night. "Far better that it be left in Yahweh's hands." She slanted a sharp look at Ruth. "You *did* say you believed in Him, that you gave Him all the credit for the coming of the caravan?"

Ruth pulled tightly on the rope that stretched a length of cloth over their sleeping mats. "Yes, Mother," she said, dutiful as a child reciting a lesson learned. "But believing in Him and feeling free to come to Him with my own problems — those are two different things."

"I don't see why."

"Belief is something that can happen in a minute," Ruth said slowly, groping for the words. "In the way that the sun can come through the clouds suddenly after a storm. But faith — that's something different. More like the almond blossoms, I guess." She smiled to show that she knew her similes were fanciful. "They grow so slowly from bud to blossom that you're hardly aware of it."

"Well, maybe." Naomi began to unroll the mats. "I guess I never had to think about it. I've always believed, and since I've been old enough, I've had faith. So I've never given it much thought."

Ruth didn't answer. Her own simile had caught at her mind. She remembered the morning she had discovered the almond blossoms, like a miracle, on the young tree. She hadn't watched them coming to maturity but suddenly, there they were.

Perhaps my faith will grow like that, she thought. If I ever have it, that is.

It was not until they lay down under the stars and silence had fallen over the camp that Ruth realized, finally and certainly, that she had left the place of her birth, that she was on her way through a strange and unknown land to a place she couldn't even imagine. The terror that shook her astonished her with its intensity. There is nothing between me and this darkness, she thought. Nothing.

Then she heard the sibilant sound of Naomi's whispering. Well, there was that, at least — Naomi's prayers, Naomi's faith. Perhaps that, with Jacob's swords, could keep her safe.

11

BY THE END of the second day, the caravan had reached the northern end of the Dead Sea. The travelers could see the lake, smoky and hazy under the shimmering heat waves that turned the water to turquoise. The women pitched their shelters while it was still light and then began to prepare the evening meal. The men lay on the ground, resting. They took turns at night keeping watch over the camp, and Ruth wondered how they endured the walking and then the watching. They seemed to be buoyed up by a burning energy. It was probably, she decided, because they were going home.

She, on the other hand, had left home. So there was no excitement to fill her, and when evening came, she was sodden with fatigue.

Naomi, apparently aware of this, looked into Ruth's face. "You're tired," she said. "Why don't you rest for a few minutes? Sit over there in the shade." When Ruth began to protest Naomi insisted, "Just this one time, you need not help us. Go, sit and look at the valley."

Grateful, Ruth walked a little way away from the group and sat down, her back against a stunted, gnarled tree. She stretched her legs and worked her toes until her feet felt easier. At first, she closed her eyes, tilting her head back against the tree, but then her curiosity about this foreign place brought her eyes open again.

The land that dropped away from this level was different

from the land she had always known. Used to the fertility of the Moab plateau with its fields of grain, its groves of olive trees, and its blossoms in the spring, she found the arid desolation in front of her both frightening and fascinating.

The setting sun threw shadows over the tawny tumble of hills, so that blue and mauve shadows shifted and changed in the small valleys and along the jutting ridges.

Surely Bethlehem would not be like this, she comforted herself. Mahlon had spoken often of the fertility of Bethlehem in the years when rain fell, and Jacob had said that he had heard that this past winter had been one of much rain. It would be impossible for her to live in a land like this one in front of her, she reflected, a land of angles and heat and emptiness. Even the lake so far below offered no hope of comfort. Although she had never seen the sea of death, Ruth had heard of its bitterness, its brackishness.

But the valley would soon be passed through, Ruth remembered, turning her head from side to side to watch the constantly changing colors of the land. Jacob planned to start out the next day as soon as it was light enough to travel, Altah had said, and they would try to get across the wide valley and over the Jordan River before the sun was too high in the sky. Fortunately it was not summer yet, and although the valley would be hot and uncomfortable, it would not be unbearable. Ruth had heard terrifying stories of the desert in the middle of summer, and she thought gratefully of their full water skins, bulging from the recent stop at a fresh spring.

A flicker of movement caught her eye. Was it simply the movement of shadows? No, it had been too rapid for that. Some small animal, perhaps, or even a larger animal that might be dangerous to a woman sitting alone even this short way beyond the security of the camp.

Alert, tense, Ruth scanned the bare slope of earth. Where had the movement been? There, behind that rock. She felt a terrible desire to get up and run back to where the fire was being built. But something held her still. If she could only control her panic, she might be able to see what it was that had moved in the dimming light. Then she could tell Jacob, and if it were a lion, the men could deal with it.

Heart pounding, she pulled herself closer to the shelter of the tree and peered, narrowing her eyes, to where she had seen the flicker of shadow or substance. If she didn't see it again, she'd know it had only been a trick of the light.

But in just a few seconds, she saw something move. A rock seemed to take on a different shape. A shaft of shadow squared itself, took on a curve. Not one animal, Ruth thought, but several of them.

As clearly as though someone had pointed out the truth to her, Ruth realized what she was seeing. It wasn't animals drifting from rock to rock, changing the shape of the shadows. It was men. Only men would know how to take advantage of the dusk in that way.

If I scream, Ruth thought, I can warn the camp. But then the creeping enemy will simply melt away and be free to attack again when we are even more vulnerable than we are now.

They surely see me, she realized. If I run, if I act frightened, they'll know that I've gone to give the warning. They'll know I've seen them.

Holding her panic down with a strength she had not known she possessed, she stretched her arms overhead, yawning widely and noisily. Then, casually, slowly, as though there were nothing on her mind more important than the desire for her supper, she got up and began to saunter back to camp. Her back felt naked and vulnerable, and it took all her courage to walk slowly, to stroll almost aimlessly along the path, to stop and admire a spike of yellow fitch blossoms growing out of the rocky soil. Slowly, indolently, she came into the area near the fire.

"Well, my cousin," she called out to Altah, taking care that her voice would carry well, "I've seen such a sunset as

I've rarely seen before. I'll help with the cleaning up since I've been lazy during the preparation of food."

Altah, looking up to give a laughing answer, stopped, puzzled, when Ruth lifted her finger to her lips.

"Try to speak normally," Ruth whispered. "Ask me to come closer."

Altah's voice was almost casual. "I was wondering where you were, and was planning to come looking for you. Here, I need your opinion on this food I'm fixing. Will you look at it?"

They bent together over the pot Altah had indicated, and Ruth spoke with hushed intensity. "Tell your lord that there are outlaws slipping up the hill toward our camp. At least, there are men, and since they're hiding behind rocks, they must be outlaws. I don't want them to know I've seen them." She raised her voice. "It looks all right to me. Perhaps a bit more meal in it? There's some in that bag over near where your lord is sleeping."

Altah nodded. "Thank you, my cousin," she said, her voice fraying a little. "I'll get some."

Ruth stood by the fire, knowing she must surely be silhouetted against the flames, but also knowing that she had to continue to act indifferent and unaware of the creeping terror out there beyond the circle of light. Darkness was falling swiftly, and in only a few minutes night would have arrived. No doubt the thieves would wait until the people had gathered around the fire to eat, their backs to the desert.

Suddenly Altah was standing beside her. "The men are sleeping," she announced clearly. "My lord roused up enough to suggest that they be allowed to sleep for a while. He even said that the women could eat first as long as we took only our share of the food."

Although Ruth could hear the tremor in Altah's voice, she was sure that strangers would never suspect the girl was anything but anxious to have her food.

The women came then, gathering around the fire, their

voices a blur of sound. Children called and crowed, and
except for the fact that the men of the caravan were still
lying on the ground beyond the light of the fire, the camp-
site must have looked normal enough, Ruth thought. She
guessed instantly what Jacob was doing. He and his men
were feigning sleep to lure in the thieves. Then, armed and
ready, they would meet the attack.

But would they be quick enough, Ruth wondered, feeling fear pulse through her body. With an effort she made
herself join the other women as they sat together, putting
the fire between themselves and the land that fell toward
the valley below.

Suddenly fierce yells splintered the night as the outlaws
rushed over the top of the hill. The women screamed in
terror, scrambling to grab the children and tumbling back to
hide among the animals.

Instantly the men of Bethlehem flew up off the ground,
swords glinting in the light of the fire, teeth showing in
savage grins. Ruth held Naomi in the curve of her arm,
hiding her face against her mother-in-law's hair as they
huddled behind a pile of rocks.

"Yahweh, help us," Naomi moaned.

If Yahweh doesn't help us, Ruth thought, wishing she
could shut her ears as effectively as she could shut her eyes,
then we're lost.

The battle was brief, bloody, and brutal. The surprisers
were surprised, and the attacked became the victorious
attackers. Six nomads were cut down, dead or dying, and if
any of the others escaped into the night, none of the Beth-
lehemites were aware of it.

At first Ruth was sickened by the killing, but gradually
she accepted the fact that if she had not acted as she had,
the thieves might have fled without harm into the desert.
She had wanted them dead. She had wanted the security of
knowing that no one was lurking in the night to menace
them. So she had no right to shudder away from the
slaughter as though she were a child.

She looked up to see Jacob standing before her. "My wife tells me that it was your courage and cleverness that saved us all."

"I — I only did what I thought I should," Ruth stammered.

"Most women would have run screaming to the fire, giving the thieves all the warning they'd need to get away."

Before Ruth could answer, he went on solemnly. "Be sure," he said, "that your good deeds will be told to our people when we get home. Be sure of that."

"Thank you," Ruth whispered.

When he had moved away, Naomi leaned close to her daughter-in-law. "I've been worried," she said. "Worried about how hard it might be for you as a foreigner in Bethlehem. I *know* how hard! Now, with Jacob's words of praise, things might be easier for you."

Ruth felt an unexpected thrust of apprehension. "You don't think your people would really be unkind to me?"

Naomi hesitated. "It's hard to say. Some might. But how can I know?" She stood up abruptly. "Come now, the men are taking up their watch. Let's try to sleep. Tomorrow's travel will be hard on all of us."

"I don't think I'll be able to sleep," Ruth said. "I'm just beginning to realize what could have happened."

"I know," Naomi agreed. "After the danger is over, you begin to think of horrible things. But you'll be all right. Here, our sleeping mat is over here."

Ruth tried to control the trembling that shook her body. She forced herself to go with Naomi to the small shelter, to take off her sandals and to lie quietly in the darkness. But every movement required an act of will. If she had allowed herself to do what she wanted to, she would have huddled cravenly close to the fire all night.

Naomi's voice came sharply through the darkness. "When we get to Bethlehem, you mustn't expect too much."

"What do you mean?" The statement startled Ruth out of her fear.

"The neighbors may mock me," Naomi admitted. "I've tried not to think about it. I've tried not to remember how bitterly they opposed our going to Moab, how they accused us of selfishness and greed. When I come back with no one, no husband, no sons, they may mock me."

"Let them mock," Ruth said. "We'll get along."

"I don't know where we'll live," Naomi said after a second of silence.

Ruth sat up. The terror of the past hour was pushed into the back of her mind. "You have no house?" she said, trying to keep the shock out of her voice. "You have no house for us to live in?"

"My lord's kinsmen would have taken it long ago."

"Surely they'll take us in," Ruth protested. "They won't make us sleep out under the sky?"

"I don't know," Naomi said. "I just don't know."

"You should have told me." The words were out before Ruth could stop them. "You should have warned me. You —"

Naomi's voice was hard. "It's not your habit to talk to me like that."

"I'm sorry," Ruth mumbled, but for a minute her anger was too hot to be suppressed. "I suppose you're going to tell me that it was your faith in Yahweh that let you lead me out so blindly. I suppose —"

Naomi interrupted again. "If I had enough faith, I wouldn't have brought up the subject at all."

"Well, if *you* don't have faith," Ruth cried, "then how am I supposed to? You're the one whose God —"

"Ruth!" The sharp words stung. "I should have told you about the house. But I didn't. So — don't blame my mistake on Yahweh."

"I'm sorry, Mother. I am." Ruth's voice shook. "Don't pay any attention to me. I'm — I'm sorry."

"It's all right," Naomi said stiffly and turned her face away.

Even if she had told me, Ruth thought, lying down again and pulling her shawl around her, it wouldn't have made any difference. It was almost as though some of Patima's common sense had entered her head. If Naomi had told her about the lack of a house sooner, it wouldn't have changed anything. Ruth would still have made her promise to Yahweh. She would still have been persuaded by her feeling for Naomi. Nothing would have changed that.

Somehow Ruth made her voice comfortable. "We'll manage," she said. "If we can travel through the desert and across the hills that lead us to Bethlehem, we won't worry about so small a thing as a house. Yahweh will provide."

She had said the words as one would say them to a child, promising sunshine even when it was raining. But to her astonishment, the words brought a comfort she had not expected. It was true. Yahweh would provide.

"Good night, Mother," Ruth said and was able, amazingly enough, to sleep without dreaming of the terror that had besieged them.

Next morning, the bodies of the thieves were dumped contemptuously into a depression and covered with a scattering of dirt.

"Let the jackals eat them," Jacob said, his voice proud.

But Ruth avoided the make-shift grave and its grisly contents. If I hadn't been under the tree dreaming over the sunset, she thought, those bodies could very well have been our bodies.

The thought shocked her. Perhaps I was meant to be there, she thought. Perhaps it was my place to be where I was so that Naomi and her people would not die. Perhaps Yahweh really used me — will use me again.

So deep was she in reflection during their descent into the valley that she was hardly aware of the thickening of the air, the slow buildup of haze between herself and the sky which had blazed above them in the early morning on the hill.

It was only when she heard the others talking about it that she pulled herself out of her pondering and began to look around her, to see and feel the heavy oppression of the valley of death. The sand burned under her sandals, and mirages danced above the smoky surface of the lake.

"Yahweh be praised that we didn't have to come through here in the middle of summer," Altah said, appearing at Ruth's elbow. "We'd all end up as skeletons along the path."

"Oh, not as bad as that," Ruth protested.

"Maybe not," Altah agreed. "But bad enough. Only two more hours, three at the most, and my lord says we'll be across the river and ready to start up the hills. The river is easy to ford this time of year, and we should be able to get far enough up out of the valley so that there will be a breath of air before we stop for the night."

"And then how long?" Ruth asked. "How long before we get to Bethlehem?"

"If nothing happens, if there are no accidents, we should make it in two more days." She slanted a quick smile at Ruth. "Does that please you, my cousin?"

"I can only hope," Ruth said slowly, remembering Naomi's confession of the night before, "that Bethlehem will shelter me."

"Don't worry." Altah's voice was warm. "By the time we finish telling our story, you'll be a heroine."

Ruth laughed in spite of her worry. "Oh, please," she begged, "not a heroine. Just a girl who will have to earn her daily bread."

"You've got nothing to worry about." Altah made an airy gesture of reassurance. "The barley harvest starts in a week or so, and every farmer in the village will need workers. Besides, as a widow, you'll be able to glean for yourself."

Ruth smiled and walked on in silence. After being the wife of the village potter, what would it be like to trudge behind the harvesters, gathering the scraps left for the poor? The only way to find out, she supposed, was to do it and see.

12

THE ROAD THAT CLIMBED westward out of the hot, desolate valley was narrow and rutted from winter rains. It twisted between jutting hills, threading its way through passes that seemed too narrow to hold a road. Occasionally, the land would drop away so that the valley could be glimpsed momentarily, and then the hills would close in again.

It seemed to Ruth, plodding upward in the dust, that the hills went on forever, fold after fold, with no promise of level fields or trees or anything that looked like home. This must be what Altah meant when she had spoken of the Wilderness of Judea, but Ruth hadn't been prepared for the vastness of the area.

Then, almost imperceptibly, tufts of green began to show along the washes where the rain had swept down the hills. As soon as there was any sign of grass, there were signs of nomads, black goatskin tents pitched in distant valleys, herds of sheep and long haired goats grazing across the land, and shy, dark men who looked away from the travelers as though they were not even there.

"At least they don't attack us," Ruth remarked with relief to Altah.

"Of course not. They're Israelites."

"And they know that this is an Israelite caravan?"

Altah's eyes slid sideways. "Well, naturally." But she did not offer any explanation.

She might think me brave, Ruth thought, and even pleasant company — at least she seems to seek me out to talk to me — but I'm still a foreigner and she's not going to trust me with any secrets of her tribe.

Hard on the heels of that thought came another one, an unexpected one. Had they kept secrets from Naomi in Moab? Had there been things which hadn't been shared even with Mahlon?

She had a quick, vivid memory of the glances she and Orpah exchanged on occasions when the worship of Chemosh had been mentioned. Yes, of course there had been Moabite traditions which had not been shared with foreigners, no matter how long they lived in Moab.

The realization was so sobering that Ruth lapsed into silence. Finally, Altah murmured some excuse and moved away. Ruth, deep in thought, hardly saw her leave. So when the caravan stopped for a midday rest, she glanced around in surprise to see the change that had taken place in the scenery. Bushes, large enough to throw shade on the ground, grew thickly along the road, and in the distance trees formed green patterns against the sky. In spite of herself, her spirits lifted a little. She could not be too distressed if there were trees and bushes wide enough to provide a shelter from the sun.

Naomi came toward Ruth, and the younger woman smiled warmly.

"Well, Mother," she said, "you hadn't told me that we would reach the trees quite so soon. Don't they look lovely up there on the hills?"

Naomi smiled, too. "You're the one who would talk about trees," she answered. "Almost any other girl would be grateful only that the men we see along the road are friends, not enemies."

"I'm grateful for that, too," Ruth said. "I'll be glad to arrive safely in Bethlehem. Will we arrive today, do you think?"

"We'll be in the Bethlehem area before nightfall, Jacob

tells me. But we'll make a camp again tonight because Jacob wants to arrive in Bethlehem in the morning."

"Did he tell you why?"

Naomi hesitated. "Not exactly, but I can guess. In the dark, there would be the immediate problem of where we're going to live. Jacob is going to have the same problem as I; he'll have to find a house. It's just better if we arrive by daylight."

Ruth unstoppered the water bottle she had been carrying and offered it to Naomi. The older woman drank and handed the bottle back. Ruth tipped it to her lips and drank deeply, grateful that there was no need now to stint on water in a land that was turning green under their feet. The water was tepid and it held the scent of the bottle, but it was wet.

Ruth took the bottle from her mouth and grinned at her mother-in-law. "I never thought, when I was drinking fresh water at the well every morning in Bezer, that I would find stale water so delicious."

"Nothing sharpens the tongue like hunger," Naomi agreed, "or in this case, thirst. The trip has been longer than I remembered, harder than I dreamed. And I've been riding a donkey most of the time. How have you endured it?"

"I tried not to think about it," Ruth said. "It was hardest in the valley, but now that I can see trees again, it's more like home."

"I should have left you in Bezer," Naomi said abruptly, ignoring Ruth's words.

"Mother, I know what you're thinking, that to take a foreign daughter-in-law into Bethlehem won't be easy, might even be unpleasant...."

A flush of shame ran up Naomi's face. "It's not that," she interrupted hastily.

But Ruth continued. "You can't boast of *anything* when you get home. Not of sons or grandsons. Only a Moabite daughter-in-law. It's all right. You don't have to pretend to me that it will be easy. I understand.

Naomi, still flushed, stared at Ruth. "You shame me,"

she muttered. "You gave up everything for me, you saved our lives when we were attacked by thieves, and I don't even act grateful."

Ruth wanted to take advantage of the confession, but her habit of submission, of keeping her feelings locked within herself was too strong, so she said nothing.

"I'll make it up to you," Naomi promised. "Somehow, when we're settled down, I'll make it up to you."

The call to move on came clearly to them. "Don't worry," Ruth said. "We'll work everything out in time. I'm sure we will."

"I hope so. Come, help me mount my donkey. We still have a long way to go."

The last part of the trip was, in some ways, the hardest for all of them. Impatience, anxiety, and fatigue weighed heavily on the whole caravan, so that they walked in silence with none of the eager conversation and laughter that had cheered the early part of the journey.

The sun was nearing the horizon when, fearful of the swift coming on of night, Jacob called everyone to a halt. As always, the women pitched the sleeping shelters and prepared the food. But this time the men did not sprawl wearily on the ground. This time, they gathered in groups to talk, and their low-voiced conversation filled the site with a hum of worry as they speculated on what their reception would be next morning.

One of the women had just declared that the food was ready when the sharp sound of hoof beats clattered through the evening.

"Donkeys," Altah cried breathlessly, "and coming from the direction of Bethlehem."

Ruth felt fear swell into her throat so that she was hardly able to breathe, and for a few minutes, the entire caravan stood in utter stillness.

Suddenly, voices could be heard, laughing voices. Surely, Ruth thought, these were not men bent on attack. No one with criminal intentions would herald his coming with laughter or allow his beasts to trot so briskly on the road's hard packed surface.

A hearty hail rang through the air. "Is this Jacob and his family from Moab? Is this my cousin approaching Bethlehem?"

Jacob spoke with quick relief. "I can't even guess, after so many years, which cousin this is, but, yes, I'm Jacob, coming home."

By that time, a small band of young men, laughing, noisy, had ridden up to where Jacob and the others stood. The leader, hardly more than a boy, slid off his donkey and ran to Jacob, embracing him warmly, kissing his cheeks.

"I'm actually related to your wife," the boy admitted to Jacob. "But since one of the caravans had brought news of your marriage to Altah, and since everyone is somehow related to everyone else in our town, I claimed cousinship."

Jacob's greeting was boisterous with relief. "No matter. I claim as cousins all men from Judah, and as brothers all men who come from Bethlehem."

The boy laughed. "Spoken like a traveler who has discovered the perils of foreign countries. Welcome, Jacob. I am Aborakim, son of Boaz. We've ridden out to bid you welcome."

The riders all dismounted with a great deal of laughter and exclamation as the men greeted one another, renewing old friendships and making new acquaintances.

Ruth, watching, was thrilled with the obvious warmth, the ready welcome. Surely these were not people who would hold a grudge against someone who had gone away in time of famine.

"See, Mother," she whispered to Naomi, "they don't seem to be holding it against Jacob that his father left Bethlehem so many years ago. It will be the same for you, I'm sure."

"Perhaps. Aborakim was a small boy when we left here. He won't even remember me."

But just then, Ruth heard Aborakim say, "Did you ride

through Bezer on your way? Did you meet my cousins, Mahlon and Chilion? My father asked me to inquire."

"We brought Mahlon's mother with us, and his widow," Jacob answered, and there was a brief silence.

"We hadn't heard," Aborakim said. "What of Chilion then?"

"Dead, too," Jacob muttered. "Naomi, their mother, is over there. Naomi, would you and Ruth come here?"

The two women came closer to the group of men. "Here, Naomi," Jacob called, "here's a boy who remembers your sons."

"And I remember him," Naomi said. "He was only a small boy when we left, but I remember how he coaxed my husband to let him make clay pots. Have you still a desire to be a potter, Aborakim?"

The boy was obviously pleased that she remembered him. "I thought my Uncle Elimelech was the greatest potter in the world. But I don't have that kind of skill. We were sorry to hear of his death so long ago. And now Jacob tells me you've had more trouble."

"My sons are both dead," Naomi said without expression. "I came back alone."

"Oh, not quite all alone," Jacob cried. "Here, Aborakim, this is Mahlon's widow, Ruth, from Moab. She's a brave woman, and when the time is right, I'll tell you of her deeds."

Aborakim looked at Ruth. "Welcome to Bethlehem," he said, but the words were flat.

He doesn't see *me*, Ruth thought. He sees a Moabite. Well, this is simply something I'll have to get used to.

"Thank you, my lord," she said.

Aborakim nodded curtly and then whirled, with a flying of robes, to cry out, "We've brought some food since you wouldn't have had time to prepare any. May we share your table and your fireside with you?"

"By all means." Jacob was hearty. "Tell me, how did you know we were coming?"

"One of the shepherd boys brought word," Aborakim began.

Ruth and Naomi slipped away from the men, and the voices faded into a murmur.

"My husband's relative," Naomi sputtered. "And he was barely civil to you."

"He's only a boy," Ruth said. "He's so full of excitement over this ride through the dusk and the privilege of being able to bid everyone welcome that he can't be bothered with strangers."

"His father would have been different," Naomi insisted. "I'm sure the boy was taught better manners."

"It doesn't matter," Ruth insisted. "Come, let's help prepare the food."

The men from Bethlehem had brought meal cakes and figs and fresh leeks. This, added to the food the women of the caravan had already prepared, gave the impression of a feast.

The women served the men and then sat quietly in the shadows, eating gratefully.

It was almost like a party, Ruth thought, looking over to where the men sat around the fire. The flames lit the dark faces with a ruddy glow and painted the robes and head coverings scarlet and saffron. The voices were excited, almost raucous. And in only a short time, the men had begun to make music by clapping and singing as the younger ones danced and stamped around the fire.

None were as merry, as flamboyant as the bright-faced Aborakim. Ruth saw the quick glances the boy cast at the few girls who were huddled, giggling, in the shadow's edge.

So it's not just strange women he dislikes, Ruth realized. He must have some special grudge against Moabites. Well, it doesn't make any difference. This son of Boaz is nothing to me, and surely there will be others in Bethlehem who will be as friendly as Jacob and Altah have been.

13

RUTH, AWAKE AT DAYBREAK, lay quietly on her pallet watching the light climb into the sky. The singing and dancing had gone on until late the night before, and then the young men from Bethlehem had bedded down with the travelers so that they could all ride into Bethlehem together.

In the lonely light of dawn, Ruth was sharply and achingly aware of her isolation in this welcoming and welcomed family. If Mahlon were alive, if he had brought her home to Bethlehem, the attitude of the people wouldn't have mattered. As Mahlon's wife, she would have had some sort of status. But she was no one's wife, and here, in this strange place, no one's daughter. Naomi had claim to her, of course, but Naomi was so filled with her own grief that she didn't seem to even think about her foreign daughter-in-law.

I wish Patima were here, Ruth thought, and could not stop the sudden tears. She turned her face away from Naomi and stifled her weeping against the scarf that she pulled over her face.

But if Patima were here, she'd have little patience with my tears, Ruth realized. She'd merely say, "You chose to come and you're here, so make the best of it." And it's true.

Oh, thank you, Yahweh, for Patima.

The small impulsive prayer bubbled out of Ruth's mind with the spontaneity of breathing. She lay in utter stillness, thinking with amazement of that small prayer. It hadn't been planned and she wasn't even sure that it was a prayer, but she had to say her gratitude to someone. And if Yahweh had made her, as Naomi claimed He had, then He must have made Patima and arranged that they be sisters.

The wonder of this idea stopped her tears as though they had never been. Yahweh is great, Ruth thought, and it's all right for me to tell Him so. Privately, in my heart, so no one else need know. I wouldn't dare ask for anything for myself, but I can praise Him. It doesn't even matter if He doesn't listen.

She gazed around at the trees taking shape in the growing light. Thank you, Yahweh, for trees and sky and grass, she thought in an ecstacy of gratitude. She had never known before that her joy over beauty could be traced to its source and shared. Her grief was lost in the singing praise that filled her.

By the time the others woke, Ruth was cheerful and ready for the day which she had believed would be one of the most frightening days of her life. She had asked Yahweh for nothing, and she had been given courage.

The caravan made its way to the huddle of the houses which made up the town of Bethlehem, and Ruth watched the homecoming in silence. She stayed close to Naomi, asking nothing, offering nothing, but her eyes darted everywhere. She saw the embraces, the tears, the laughter.

And she saw the amazement on the faces of the women who crowded up to Naomi.

"Can this be Naomi?" they cried.

Ruth could understand why they were questioning the fact of Naomi's identity. She had been only middle-aged when she had left Bethlehem, a strong woman surrounded by her husband and her two sons. Now she was worn, tired, grieved, and old. No wonder they hardly knew her.

"Don't even call me Naomi," Naomi cried. "Naomi means delight, but there is no delight in me. I had everything when I left you, a husband, sons, and hope for grandsons. Now I'm empty, barren, so call me Mara for the bitterness which fills me. The Almighty has dealt bitterly with me. He has brought me home empty."

A few of the women pulled away from the stinging tirade, but others, compassion in their faces, pushed closer to her.

"But at least you've come home," one of them cried. "You're not alone any longer."

Gratefully, Naomi went into the arms opened for her comfort. Ruth, standing awkwardly on the outskirts of the circle, looked up to meet the mocking glance of Aborakim. He didn't say anything, but his expression was plainer than words.

She can't think much of you, his eyes were proclaiming, if she never even mentioned you. Even to her, you're an outsider.

For a few seconds, Ruth winced away from the boy's scorn, but then she remembered the praise that had filled her at dawn. She couldn't be totally unworthy or Yahweh would not have granted her an awareness of His power. She forced herself to stand erect, staring resolutely at the boy. In the end, his eyes were the ones to drop.

Holding her head high, Ruth moved closer to the women and was rewarded with Naomi's sudden cry of, "Ruth. I nearly forgot you. Come, my dear."

Looking up, Ruth saw that Aborakim had heard, and she saw with satisfaction the faint tinge of pink on his cheeks.

But I don't want an enemy, Ruth thought, and forced herself to smile her friendliest smile at him before she turned to follow Naomi and her family and friends.

The rest of that day was simply a blur of faces and names, new sensations, and odd customs. Naomi's sister, Elena, also a widow, told them they were welcome to stay for a day or so with her at her son's house. The house was so crowded with small children that Ruth knew they could not stay long, but at least for now they could rest in the knowledge that there would be a roof over their heads.

Late in the afternoon, Altah appeared suddenly, and

Ruth, sitting alone, looked up to see her beckoning from the edge of the yard.

"Can you come here for a minute?" Altah asked. "I have some news for you. Exciting news."

Ruth got up quickly. "Of course. What is it?"

"Everyone has been so good," Altah confided. "Everyone in the caravan has found a place to stay, either with family or in some old, empty houses in the town. My lord and I will be living with some cousins on the edge of town."

"That's wonderful," Ruth said. "This is the home of my mother-in-law's nephew and they've made us welcome, but there simply isn't enough room for two more women. I imagine we'll have to start looking for a room somewhere tomorrow. I don't know what we'll use for payment. Perhaps we could sell the donkey —"

Altah interrupted. "But that's what I came to tell you. On the back of the lot where we'll live there's an old shed, but it's made of stone and if the roof is repaired, I think you and Naomi could live in it."

"Truly?"

"Yes, it belongs to my husband's family, but no one seems to have any use for it. I think it was used as a stable at one time. It needs a lot of cleaning."

"That's no problem," Ruth said. "No one can wedge clay for years and be afraid of hard work. But, you mean, we can use it without paying?"

"For the time being." Altah's voice was comfortable. "Maybe later, when you are better fixed than you are now, there will be a small rent. But if you can get Naomi's family to fix the roof (surely you'll admit you need a man for that?), and if you and Naomi can clean the inside, then it's yours."

"Oh, Altah!" Ruth had to clench her hands together to keep from embracing the girl facing her.

But Altah had no such qualms. She threw her arms around Ruth and hugged her. "It will be lovely to have you so close," she said. "When my baby is born — if Yahweh grants me safe delivery — than you can be an aunt."

Ruth, afraid to risk her voice, returned the hug with gratitude.

"And as soon as the place is decent enough to live in," Altah said, "the barley will be ripe, and you can glean all the grain you'll need for the two of you to eat."

"But paying for it may be hard," Ruth demurred.

"Don't you remember? I told you before that the harvesters are required to leave the corners of every field unharvested, so that widows and orphans can glean all they want."

"I can't believe it." Ruth's laugh was shaky. "All my problems solved at once."

"I'm glad," Altah said. "But now I've got to hurry back. My lord told me to come to tell you about the shed, but he didn't say I could stand and chat."

They exchanged a rueful smile. "I'll see you at the well most mornings," Ruth suggested. "Surely that part of life is just the same as it is in Moab?"

"I can't imagine a place anywhere on the earth that women wouldn't have to carry water," Altah said. "So, I'll see you then."

When Ruth came back into the yard, the women all stopped talking long enough to look at her with curiosity.

"What did Altah want?" Naomi asked.

"Wonderful news, Mother," Ruth cried. "She and her lord have found a little shed where you and I can live. We'll have to crowd your nephew and his family out of their beds only long enough for the roof to be repaired and the debris cleaned out. Then we can move into it."

Everyone talked at once, and when Ruth explained that the shed stood on the property where Jacob and Altah would live with cousins, Elena spoke up quickly.

"I remember the place well. Old Eli built it for some favorite sheep, and there were those who said he was crazy to work with stones for animals. Now, it will shelter you."

"You see," someone said, "Yahweh does care for you."

"He chastens *and* provides," Naomi admitted. "But our

fathers never told us we could have one without the other."

"Not and be a woman," Elena said.

And no one added, "Especially a woman from a foreign land," but Ruth felt it in the glances that slid her way.

The following day, Naomi and Ruth went to see the small shed that Altah had said would be theirs. It was in a field which had been grazed almost to the ground by sheep, but it was sheltered by a huge fig tree. The broad green leaves moved softly in the morning air, and the dappled shade lay like a blessing over the tiny building.

The two women stood looking into the interior. A small window in one wall and a considerably larger break in the roof allowed enough light to enter that they could make out the piles of debris that cluttered the floor. If either of them felt any dismay, they did not allow it to show in their faces or their voices.

"We can go ahead and scrub and clean," Ruth said briskly. "The winter rains are finished, so the hole in the roof will let in only sunlight and starlight."

"Or a wandering animal," Naomi began doubtfully.

"Not with the smell and sound of people inside," Ruth insisted. "Besides, look how close it is to the house where Jacob and Altah will be living. We could only have to scream once, and a man would be here to kill whatever has to be killed."

Naomi looked at her and smiled. "You've changed," she said slowly. "Once, you wouldn't have thought of the practical side of things. You're beginning to sound almost like Patima."

Ruth nodded. "I know. It's as though I've acquired some of Patima's good sense. While I lived near her, I guess I didn't need it, but now...." She spread her hands, her usual reticence rendering her inarticulate.

"Well," Naomi began briskly, "I suppose we'd better start cleaning this out. Talking will never bring order to a messy place."

Ruth pulled her robe a little higher and tightened the girdle around her waist. "You're right," she agreed. "If you'll find a branch and some twigs to make a broom, I'll begin by carrying out the debris."

She found, as she worked, that most of the accumulation on the floor was litter from the roof. It was dirty and unpleasant to carry out, but the satisfaction of seeing order grow out of chaos was enormous.

They discovered some sheep-shearing equipment, and this they carried to the owner's house. Altah met them at the door.

"I feel I should be helping you," she announced, "but my lord's cousin has asked me to watch the little ones while she helps her lord in the fields. The barley has done well this year, and there is need for many hands. But someone has to watch the children."

"It's better for the child you carry that you don't do so much stooping," Naomi said.

"And don't worry about not helping us," Ruth added. "You've done more than enough in finding us a place to stay. The work is pleasant in the shade of the tree, and we're enjoying it. Or at least I am."

"I, too," Naomi said. "What woman would find it hard to make a home?"

"What about the roof?" Altah asked anxiously.

"It needs repair," Ruth admitted, "but maybe we can make do until after the harvest time."

The look Altah gave her was approving. "If you could manage, I know the men would appreciate it. They'll be working from dawn until dark, I'm told."

"Don't worry," Ruth said. "We'll be fine."

"It's a good thing," Naomi confided as they walked back to the shed, "that we brought pots and sleeping mats from Bezer. At least we have dishes to eat from and something to sleep on."

"There are several shelves built into the walls," Ruth told her. "I suppose the builder — did Elena say his name was

Eli? — put them there to hold supplies for the sheep. They seem strong and sturdy and we ought to be able to use them to hold our jars and bowls and pots."

"It won't be like the house in Bezer," Naomi began.

"But it will be ours," Ruth said. "Just ours. We won't need to depend on anyone else."

"Well, that's true," Naomi admitted. "As long as you're not discontented."

"I'm fine," Ruth insisted and ducked her head to enter the low door.

A movement inside brought a quick breathless gasp from her. She saw instantly that a man was standing in the room, and almost at once she recognized Aborakim.

"You startled me, my lord," she stammered. "Were you looking for my mother-in-law?"

"Yes. My father sent me to talk to her."

"Aborakim?" Naomi was still standing in the doorway. "Come out in the sun where I can see you."

The boy moved toward her. "My father sends his greetings and wants to know if there's anything he can do to help you."

Naomi's face revealed her pleasure. "How good of him. Please tell him how grateful we are. But I don't think we need anything."

Aborakim looked over his head. "Not even someone to repair your roof?"

"Well, yes, that," Naomi conceded. "But as Ruth points out, the winter rains are past, and we can wait until the barley harvest is over when the men will have more free time."

Aborakim ignored her reference to Ruth. "Father will probably send his servants to repair the roof soon. As kinsman to your husband, he feels responsible."

Naomi smiled. "And we appreciate it."

"Will the place suit?" Aborakim asked, looking disdainfully at the tiny room, still dirty and unswept.

"Oh, yes. Ruth and I will have it fixed up in no time. Wait and see."

Still the boy gave no indication that he was even aware of Ruth's presence. "I'll tell my father," he offered. "He'll be glad you're all right, and no doubt his servants will be over soon."

He strode across the field, and Naomi stood looking after him, her forehead creased in a scowl.

"Why is he so rude to you?" she asked suddenly, turning to Ruth. "You've done nothing to offend him."

"I'm a Moabite," Ruth reminded her. "Some people are more, well, more sensitive to this than others. You've said so yourself."

"He's spoiled," Naomi muttered. "His father or mother should teach him better."

"I think Altah said his mother was dead. The day we met in Bezer she mentioned that her aunt, who had been married to a man named Boaz, was dead." Ruth began to sweep the cleared portion of the floor with her twig broom. "I imagine she meant Aborakim's mother. I could be wrong."

"Well, no matter," Naomi said. "I never knew her well. It was his father, Boaz, who was related to my lord Elimelech. But the boy is still rude."

"Most boys that age think they have a right to be rude," Ruth murmured almost absently.

"I'm going for water," Naomi said. "We can start scrubbing. In two days we ought to have the place ready to stay in. Especially if they should really come to fix the roof."

"And when we have a solid roof over our heads, we won't have anything to worry about except getting food to eat."

Naomi paused in the doorway. "And speaking of that," she began.

Ruth's voice was very casual. "I'm sure that things are the same here as they are in Moab. It's the duty of childless women to go out to find food. If you'll carry the water each day and grind the meal, I'll go out to gather barley."

Still, Naomi looked a little doubtful. "As my son's wife, you didn't have to do such menial work."

"But as your son's widow," Ruth said, making her voice

cheerful, "I have a duty to feed us. Surely nothing so very dreadful can happen to me in the barley fields."

"Yahweh will have to protect you," Naomi muttered in a voice that was anything but comforting.

She hurried away toward the well, and Ruth stood for a minute looking after, hearing the worry in Naomi's voice and feeling a similar worry in her own mind. I won't even think about it, Ruth decided, and turned to her sweeping.

part III

And Ruth the Moabitess said to Naomi, "Please let me go to the field and glean." ...So she departed and went and gleaned in the field after the reapers; and she happened to come to...the field belonging to Boaz, who was of the family of Elimelech.   Ruth 2: 2*a*, 3

14

IT TOOK TWO DAYS of continuous labor before the rough, dirty little shed was fit to live in. Using mud, Naomi and Ruth filled in the broken chinks between the stones, they swept and smoothed the dirt floor, they scrubbed the inside walls and the wooden shelves and even spread a little whitewash that was given them on the walls. Toward the end of the second day, two men, announcing that they were servants of Boaz, came to repair the roof. Gratefully, the women watched as the sagging, weakened roof was quickly and skillfully restored.

The hut was much darker after the roof was repaired, but they were used to that. The dimness created an aura of security. They put oil in the small clay bowl that held a woven wick, lit it from the lamp in Altah's house, and then placed it on a shelf in the corner where it would be least likely to be knocked over. Barring accident or carelessness, the lamp would never go out.

"There!" Ruth said when the lamp was shedding its small light in the room. "Now, I'm beginning to feel as though it were truly a home."

"Thanks to Boaz," Naomi said. "When his servants left, I asked them to express our gratitude to him. I'll sleep better knowing that nothing will drop on me from a hole in the roof."

"He must be very kind," Ruth murmured, intent on

finding just the right place to put the rolled sleeping mats.

"I didn't know him well, but my lord Elimelech always spoke highly of him. He has two sons, I think. You've met Aborakim, but I'm sure you're not impressed. The younger one is Chalem, I think. He's only a child."

Ruth hardly listened. A dozen times she had started to ask a question that had burned in her for several days, but always she had decided the time wasn't right for it. Now her concern had grown to the point where it could no longer be ignored.

"Mother," she began, "the other day when we first found this place, when we talked of the possibility of my going out into the fields, you acted as though I would be in danger, and yet you always boasted in Moab that there was never anything like the fertility rites in your own country. You acted as though things like that only happened in Moab."

Naomi looked at Ruth. "Well, only in Moab is such action approved. Not only approved but encouraged. Such a thing would be considered terrible here."

"But," Ruth persisted, "you think it *could* happen? A woman, an unprotected woman, might be — might be molested in the fields?"

"It's been known to happen," Naomi conceded.

Ruth's voice was anxious. "But aren't all people here followers of Yahweh? Would Yahweh permit such a thing?"

"Of course not," Naomi retorted. "Yahweh would condemn it. But even people who claim to be followers of Yahweh sometimes disobey the law."

Ruth made a hopeless gesture with her hands. "Then it really isn't any different here than it was in Moab?"

"I didn't say that! In Moab there were orgies. Here such acts are considered a sin. The man would be punished."

"Even if the victim were a foreigner?" Ruth asked.

Naomi's eyes shifted and slid away from Ruth's. "How do I know? If I could prevent your having to go into the fields, you know I would."

Ruth felt a sense of futility. Protest, arguments, and fear all shaped words she wanted to say. But there was no use upsetting Naomi. Nothing was going to be changed.

"It's all right, Mother," Ruth said. "Let's not think about it."

"How can I help thinking about it?" Naomi fretted. "Isn't it bad enough just to know that here you'll be forced to eat the inferior bread made from barley while in your own country you had bread made of wheat? How do you think I feel that you must go out unprotected and then come home to poor food?"

"It's what I chose," Ruth said stubbornly. Deliberately, she changed the subject. "What did I see the servants of Boaz bringing? They were surely carrying more than clean thatch. One of them was almost bent to the ground with the load in his hands."

"They brought a small quern for grinding our grain," Naomi answered. "I told them to put it near the tree in the shade. If you're able to bring grain home tomorrow, we'll be able to grind it and make cakes for eating. Elena gave us some olives and a bit of goat cheese. We'll manage, I guess."

"Of course we will. We can use rocks heated in a fire to bake the cakes on. Until we get an oven made, that is. I wish we had some of the good clay from Bezer to build an oven."

Naomi smiled. "We'll even have an oven in time, Yahweh willing."

The women ducked their heads and came out of the low door. The land on which the hut stood was high, and a gentle breeze moved the leaves of the fig tree. Although the sun was brilliant and hot, the shade moved with a caressing touch to the skin.

"There," Naomi said and pointed. "That land over there. Can you see the row of stones along the edge of the hill? That's the land of my lord Elimelech."

Ruth stared at her mother-in-law in astonishment. "But you said his kinsmen would have taken it."

"The house, yes. Not the land. They might use it, but the land still belongs to the sons of Elimelech. It's mine now to be held in trust for future sons. But the wise thing to do would be to sell it, I suppose. We'd earn enough to keep us for a while."

"Could you do that?"

Naomi nodded. "I think so. To a kinsman, of course. To one of my lord's kinsmen. I'll have to look into it."

Ruth looked across the slope of sheep bitten fields to where the stones marked the land of Elimelech. If she had borne a son, she thought with a grief that never wholly left her, that land would belong to him. Even though he were an infant, the land and its promise would be his. Perhaps as the mother of a land owner, she would not have to face the idea that next morning she would have to start going into the barley fields.

But, said the element of Patima that never seemed to leave her now, she didn't have a son. She had no reason to hope that she would ever have a son. That kind of joy was too unattainable to even become part of her dreams.

"Then I hope you'll be able to sell it," Ruth said in so calm a voice that Naomi would never know how her thoughts had traveled. "Now let's fix our evening meal. Tomorrow may be difficult."

"I'll pray for your safety," Naomi promised. "All the time you're away from home, I'll be praying that Yahweh will hold you safely in His hands."

I suppose I can't expect Yahweh to answer *all* of Naomi's prayers, Ruth thought with a touch of wryness. She stood, alone and ignored, on the edge of a field watching the men and women who worked and laughed and sang. Or maybe, her thoughts went on, to be held in Yahweh's hand is just to be safe, not necessarily happy.

She had never felt so solitary in her life, even though she was surrounded by people. No one spoke to her or asked her to join them. A leper would hardly be more alone, Ruth thought with sudden bitterness.

Altah's friendliness had not prepared her for this kind of discrimination. Altah had smiled and talked, sharing her feelings and her good fortune. Altah had acted as though it didn't make any difference that Ruth had been born in Moab.

And why not? Ruth almost heard the sound of Patima's voice. Altah, herself, had been a foreigner. She understood. Most of her life she had lived in a land where she had been an outsider. And even she had been amazed that Moabites loved their families with the same warmth that Israelites loved theirs.

So, then, I'm a foreigner, Ruth decided, and no one is going to be friendly to me as long as I stand here on the edge of the field sulking and feeling sorry for myself.

She squared her shoulders, loosening her shawl so she could use one end of it for carrying grain, and forced herself to approach one of the men who was acting as overseer.

"Pardon me," Ruth said, "may I glean in this field?"

The man narrowed his eyes as he gazed at her. "You have an accent," he announced as though it were a blemish. "And I don't know you. What are you doing in my field?"

"I'm the daughter-in-law of Naomi, widow of Elimelech. She has just returned from Moab and she brought me with her." Ruth spoke sturdily enough, but her heart began to hammer as the fellow raked her up and down with his bold, dark eyes.

"I know no one named Naomi," he drawled, moving closer to her.

"I assure you, my lord, we came in the caravan with Jacob, son of Mishrah. May I glean?"

Suddenly the man laughed, tipping back his head as though he were highly amused. "Why not? Glean if you will. It ought to keep you in this field until dusk."

Ruth felt a thrust of apprehension. "Thank you, my lord," she whispered, her mind already busy with plans to run as soon as she had reached the far side of the field.

"And mind you." The man's voice was rough. "I'll be watching you. Don't try to go to anyone else's field. At least not until I've collected my fee."

Ruth turned away, filled with both anger and fear. He had no right; the man had no right. Ah, but he had the right of power, she thought. He was the overseer in this field, and she was a poor foreigner, alone, with no one to whom she could turn. She glanced over her shoulder toward the overseer and saw his dark, hungry eyes staring at her, holding her as tightly as though she were bound with ropes.

If Naomi would only walk out to see where I am, Ruth thought with despair. Or if Altah or Jacob would happen to go by. If even Elena or her son were near, I could call on them. But there is no one. No one.

The sun was already hot, although the morning was still new. Ruth, painfully aware of the overseer's eyes, moved slowly across the field. To add to her despair, she saw that the other women were greedily grabbing as much of the grain as possible from the wake of the reapers. She tried to tell herself that they were probably as much in need of food as she was, but she found no solace in the reminder.

The continuous bending over in the sun, often to pick up only single stalks of barley, sent sharp pains through Ruth's back, and thirst parched her tongue. For a few minutes she allowed herself to think of the feel of cool clay in her hands, to remember the jars of cool water standing in every corner of the pottery. Then, resolutely, she put such thoughts aside and tried to concentrate on the task at hand.

A clump of barley, dropped from the reaper's hands after his sickle had cut it from the stalk, lay almost at her feet. Grateful for the size of the pile of grain, she stooped to get it. A quick shove caused her to lose her balance, and as she staggered, she saw another woman reach to gather the grain.

Awkwardly, Ruth regained her balance and turned to stare at the woman who had jostled her aside. As she hesitated, afraid to express the anger that scalded through her, a small voice piped up clearly.

"You had no right to do that," the voice shrilled while a

grubby hand pointed to Ruth. "This woman was reaching for it first."

Ruth looked down into the angry face of a boy no more than ten years old.

"Thank you," Ruth said, surprised, "but it's all right."

"Why is it all right?" The boy glared up at her, as angry, it seemed, at her leniency as he was at the other woman's piracy.

"Well, there's no point in creating a fuss." Ruth looked around uneasily. "I don't want to make anyone angry."

The boy continued to stare. "You're a foreigner, aren't you? You have an accent."

Ruth nodded with a feeling of hopelessness. Even the very young, she thought wearily.

"From where?" If there was anything in the boy's voice, it was eagerness. "Edom? Moab? Egypt?"

To her own amazement, Ruth laughed. "Not Egypt. Egyptians don't speak the language you and I do. I might sound as though I had an accent, but at least we speak the same words."

"Where then?"

"Moab."

"Oh." He looked a little disappointed. "I was hoping maybe Egypt or Mesopotamia. I was going to ask you a lot of questions. But Aborakim says Moab is —" He caught himself, apparently remembering his manners. "Moab is not so different, I guess," he added politely.

But her attention had caught on one word. "Aborakim?"

"My brother. See, those are our fields over there. I'm supposed to be picking up the smaller sheaves, but one of the boys over here threw a stone at me. I came looking for him."

"Did you find him?" Her fear of the overseer had almost melted away in this small conversation, in the comfort of being accepted as just another person.

"He hid, the coward," the boy said, scorn coloring his voice. "But I'd better get back. Why don't you come along?

There aren't too many gleaning in our fields, and my father's very generous."

"I don't know," Ruth began, glancing over her shoulder at the overseer who had become her jailer.

The boy's eyes followed hers. "What's it to old Marak where you glean? I'll tell him you're coming with me. I'll tell him my father's expecting us." The glance he threw her was wicked. "It won't be a lie. My father is expecting *me*."

Ruth watched the boy run over to Marak and begin to talk. The overseer's face was black and surly, but the boy was casual, his words tumbling out in what must have been a persuasive flow. In only a few minutes, the child was back beside her.

"Let's go," he said, offering no explanation of what he'd said.

Did she dare leave? Was she protected enough by the innocence and friendliness of the child who stood impatiently beside her. Naomi's promise ran through her like fire. "All the time you're gone from home, I'll be praying that Yahweh will hold you in His hand."

Ruth straightened her shoulders, hardly feeling the pain. "Well, then," she said, smiling down at the boy, "we'll go."

Without even a backward glance, she turned to follow the boy out of the field where fear had imprisoned her. There was no call, no reprimand as they walked together toward the fields of Boaz.

15

THE BOY'S NAME was Chalem, he confided to Ruth as they made their way to his father's fields, and as soon as they arrived, he ran to the man who was overseeing the reapers. After only a few words, Ruth was rewarded with a nod and gesture from the man which indicated she was free to glean. There was none of the greedy lust she had seen in Marak's eyes, so her heart was grateful as she turned away to start work.

Chalem, with a cheerful wave, ran toward a distant corner of the field. "I'll talk to you later," he flung over his shoulder. "Will you tell me about Moab?"

"Of course," she answered and felt herself smiling as she stooped for the grain.

She was astonished to discover, as the morning went on, that several of the gleaners smiled at her and one or two even spoke to her. What was even more important, none of the men did anything to frighten her.

There was something in this place, she decided, that she had not found in the other one. She had no idea what it was; she was only grateful for the absence of fear, for the presence of even a small degree of kindness.

As the sun rose higher, she got hotter and hotter. In spite of her resolution not to think of the days in Bezer, she could not help but remember the cool shade of the pottery, the dampness that had emanated from the bins of wet clay. Her tongue seemed to cleave to the roof of her mouth and she wondered why she had been so foolish as to come out into the fields without a water skin. Naomi should have known better, at least.

Chalem flashed by with a wide grin and another wave of his skinny brown arm. "There's water in the shed over there," he called. "You're welcome to go over for some any time."

She smiled her gratitude and then turned hesitantly to the woman beside her.

"Is it really all right? I thought if there was any water, it would be for the hired laborers."

The woman straightened slowly while a grimace of pain crossed her face. "In some fields, yes. Boaz is very kind. That's why I always try to come to his fields."

"You mean, I can just go over and drink?" Ruth asked.

"Yes, I'll go with you. My mouth feels like a desert."

"I've just crossed the desert," Ruth admitted, "so I know just exactly what you mean." She ran her tongue across her lips. "My name is Ruth. I'm the daughter-in-law of Naomi."

The woman hesitated so briefly that it could almost be called no hesitation at all. "And I'm Shiri, the widow of Aaron. I understand you've come from Moab."

"Yes."

Shiri looked at her with curiosity. "Are you happy here?"

Ruth shrugged. "When one is a widow, happiness is something one hardly thinks about, let alone hopes for. I'm content. I'm where I think I ought to be."

Shiri smiled. "Here, let's pile our grain under our shawls. That way, no one will take it. Then we'll go for water."

"Does the presence of a shawl make it safe?"

"It marks the grain as ours. Especially in the fields of good men."

Ruth laid her bundle on the ground. She had tried to pick up only the stalks which had ripe heads of grain, so the bundle was small. But the grain was full and heavy; when she and Naomi had threshed it and separated it from the chaff, there would be enough for a loaf of bread. And then tomorrow if she were lucky, she could gather enough for another loaf.

"Then, come," Shiri said, and they walked toward the patch of shade under the thatched roof of the shelter which had been erected for the harvesters.

Several of the hired workers were standing in the shed, waiting for their turn at the water jar. Their skin was dark from constant exposure to the sun, and the women's hands were as rough and coarse as the men's. It occurred to Ruth that this might be her future. It was all very well that widows and orphans were allowed the privilege of gleaning for their daily bread during the harvest, but what about the days that came after harvest? What about seed time and winter and the rainy season? If she and Naomi were to live with any degree of comfort or ease, she would have to do more than follow the reapers. She would have to earn or buy or harvest enough grain to fill their storage jars for the months between harvests. Well, time enough to worry about that later. For now, the generosity of a law that allowed her to gather even a little grain would make life possible for them.

"The hired women are always married," Shiri said almost as though she could read Ruth's thoughts. "Their husbands are always in the fields with them. I don't think anyone would hire widows."

Ruth looked at her with dismay. "Then how do widows survive? Surely we can't gather up enough grain to keep us during the year. What do you do?"

Shiri shrugged. "Some widows have a father or brother who will help them out. Some have sons, and they don't have to worry at all. Some are forced to beg. I, myself, I hope for a go'el."

"A go'el? I don't know the word."

"A kinsman-redeemer. A brother-in-law or cousin, a cousin of your husband, that is, who will marry you and give you a home and, if Yahweh grants it, even give you a son. Isn't it like that in Moab?"

"I've heard of the custom," Ruth said evasively, thinking

of the bitterness she had suffered at the thought of sharing
Mahlon with Orpah. How willingly she would share now,
she thought with longing, if she could have the security
and peace of that life in Bezer again. "I wish you well," she
added politely.

"My father-in-law is trying to make the arrangements.
There have already been several meetings of the men at the
city gate. I hope it'll be settled soon."

"You have children?"

"No, of course not. If I had, there would be no need for
a go'el. It's because there was no son to carry on my
husband's name..."

"I know. I have no son either."

They had reached the water jar. Shiri dipped the gourd
into the water and held it out to Ruth. "Here," she said.
"Drink."

The gesture of friendship was so unexpected that Ruth
felt a quick stinging in her eyes. "Thank you," she whispered and lifted the dripping gourd to her lips.

When Shiri had drunk, she pointed to a place in the
shade. "Here," she said. "Let's sit for a minute or two. No
one will touch our grain, and I don't know about you, but I
need a bit of rest."

Ruth sank gratefully to the shaded ground. She glanced
around to see if there were any signs that she was not
welcome, but no one seemed to be paying any attention to
her.

"There she is," an eager little voice cried out, and Ruth
looked up to see Chalem coming toward her. He was tow-
ing someone behind him, and she saw that it was Aborakim. "See," the boy announced. "I told you there was
someone from Moab here. I made her welcome."

Aborakim looked at Ruth as she got hastily to her feet.
"My lord," she said and bent her head. "I'm more grateful
to your brother than I can say."

"How did you know he was my brother?" Chalem cried.

"We've met before," Ruth said.

Aborakim inclined his head slightly. "My little brother

has acquired the idea that if someone is from another land, he — or she — is somehow special."

A dozen retorts trembled on Ruth's tongue. "A false idea, of course," she murmured. "He'll find as he gets older that all people are pretty much the same."

"You think so?" Aborakim's color was high. "I haven't found it so."

"Truly, my lord?" Ruth kept her voice even.

"My best friend was murdered by a Moabite," Aborakim said, biting off the words. "For no reason. He was in Moab to do some trading. He went in peace, and they murdered him."

Ruth moved her hands helplessly. "I'm sorry, my lord."

"But it's not *her* fault," Chalem clamored. "She wasn't the one who killed him."

"She's a Moabite," Aborakim said. "I hate all Moabites."

Chalem looked from Ruth to Aborakim, his face scarlet with embarrassment. Suddenly there was a sound of clattering hooves, and Ruth looked up to see several donkeys trotting toward them. The man on the first beast was middle-aged, but he sat his beast as though he were a leader of men. His shoulders were straight, his head high, and his face serene.

"It's Father," Chalem shouted. "It's Father." Ignoring Ruth and Aborakim, he raced away from the shed and flung himself toward the man who was approaching. Ruth saw the man's face as he greeted his son and she was touched by the instant pride and gladness that lit the widely spaced dark eyes and turned up the corners of the full lipped mouth.

"You look like your father, my lord," Ruth said, not even realizing that she was ignoring Aborakim's declaration of hatred.

"As you say." Aborakim's voice was cold.

Too late Ruth realized her error. She had spoken to him as to an equal, as to a friend. "I'm sorry, my lord," she whispered and backed away from him.

With a contemptuous toss of his head, Aborakim turned from her and strode toward the place where Chalem and his father were greeting each other with such delight.

"He shouldn't have been so rude," Shiri said, her embarrassment as obvious as Chalem's had been. "We try to teach our children to be more courteous than that. Of course he doesn't think of himself as a child."

"He's kin to my father-in-law," Ruth explained. "I think he feels a great sense of, well, outrage, that someone related to him, even if only through marriage, should have brought a Moabite here to Bethlehem. My mother-in-law has been very upset. But since he told about his friend's death, I understand a little better."

"I remember the story," Shiri said. "Aborakim and Joash, the boy who was killed, had been friends since childhood. It was a very sad thing. He, Aborakim that is, probably vowed himself to vengeance. You know how boys are."

"Yes, I know. I'm only surprised the little one doesn't copy his brother."

Shiri laughed. "Not Chalem. He's exactly like his father, gentle and merry. He wouldn't have the least idea how to go about being vengeful."

"I wonder what makes them so different," Ruth murmured, turning to watch the man, Boaz, and his sons.

She was in time to see Boaz lift his arm in greeting as two of the hired men came toward the shed. "May the Lord be with you," Boaz cried out in a hearty voice.

"And may Yahweh bless you, my lord," the men answered, smiling broadly.

Ruth stood very still. That must be what made the difference between this field and the first one, she reflected. Naomi had said that although all men who lived in this land were children of Yahweh, not all of them followed His law. This man, Boaz, must be one of those who followed the law, one of those who bore the mark of his God in his daily life. She sat down again and smiled at Shiri. "Shall we rest a little longer?" she suggested, "before we go back to glean?"

Boaz slid down from his donkey and smiled with affection at his younger son. "Have you been working as I told you?"

"Most of the time," Chalem said. "I met a Moabite, but Aborakim doesn't like her."

"The daughter-in-law of Naomi?" Boaz inquired of Aborakim.

The older boy's face was surly. "Yes, Father. They say her name is Ruth. I've tried not to talk to her."

Boaz sighed. Turning to Chalem he said, "And where did *you* meet her?"

"In the field of Marak. She seemed sad or worried. I invited her to come into our fields. Marak acted angry, but she was glad to come."

Boaz lifted his head. "What do you mean, glad to come?"

Chalem frowned with concentration. "I can't explain it any other way. She just seemed glad."

"A stranger," Boaz murmured to Aborakim. "A stranger in a strange land. A woman hasn't much protection from men like Marak."

Aborakim shrugged his shoulders. "She's a Moabite," he said. "What difference does it make?"

"The widow and the orphan are our responsibility." Boaz' voice was stern. "You know the law."

"Yes, Father," Aborakim said, but his voice was hard.

"She's going to tell me about her country," Chalem offered. "If I ever have a chance to talk to her, she is."

"Then you'll learn something you don't know now," Boaz said. "You could do far worse than talk to her. I understand she's a heroine."

"A heroine?" Chalem's voice slid up in delight and Aborakim's scaled as high with incredulity.

Boaz nodded. "Indeed. I got it from Jacob, the son of Mishrah, who has only recently returned from Moab. They were attacked by desert thieves, and only Ruth's coolheadedness saved them from certain death."

"I knew it," Chalem said with satisfaction. "I knew she was different."

Aborakim made no comment and Boaz went on. "Not only that, but she has come here out of a sense of loyalty and duty toward her mother-in-law. Jacob speaks very highly of her."

"Then I was wise to invite her to our fields, wasn't I?" Chalem asked.

"Yes, very wise. If Marak had in his mind what I suspect he had, you did her a great favor."

"I don't understand." Chalem looked puzzled.

"Never mind. It's enough that she's safely in this place. Aborakim, go and tell the men she is not to be molested in these fields. Not at any time or under any circumstances."

For a few seconds, the boy's anger burned hotly in his eyes. But his father's steady gaze finally forced him into a reluctant submission.

"Yes, Father," he muttered.

"I'll trust you to carry out my orders exactly," Boaz said.

"Have I ever deceived you?" Aborakim demanded.

"No. That's why I can give you an unwelcome task and expect you to carry it out."

A strange mixture of irritation and pride struggled on the boy's face, but in the end it was pride which won. "You know I would do anything for you, Father," he said.

"I know." The hand Boaz dropped on his son's shoulder was very gentle. "I thank Yahweh daily for such sons as I have."

Aborakim bent his head and turned to carry out his father's orders.

Chalem watched him go. "He didn't want to do it," he said. "Why didn't he?"

"It doesn't matter why," Boaz said. "It's enough that he does what I ask even against his wishes. Now, come, let's go over to the shed and see how the work is going."

"And meet my friend, Ruth?" The boy's voice was eager.

Boaz smiled. "And meet your friend, Ruth."

16

FROM WHERE SHE SAT on the ground, Ruth watched Boaz and his sons. The man's goodness and authority were evident even though she could not hear the words that were spoken.

"What a pity his wife is dead," Ruth murmured to Shiri. "He's obviously a good father; he must have been a good husband. His wife would have been fortunate."

Shiri made a sound of assent. "There are many women in Bethlehem who would like to have him for a husband. Young widows, even unmarried girls. He doesn't seem to be in a hurry to make such a decision."

"No doubt his sons ease his loneliness."

"No doubt. Aborakim is an arrogant boy, but evidently he doesn't give his father any trouble. Or at least that's what the servants say. Better an obedient son than a loving one."

Ruth looked at her in astonishment. "What a strange thing to say."

"But true," Shiri insisted. "A loving son can wind his arms around your neck and his words around your heart and then go off and do things you've forbidden him to do."

"I suppose." Ruth sounded dubious. In her mind she was seeing again that day in their house in Bezer when she had declared her devotion to Naomi. "Wherever you go, I will go," she had said. But had she said it out of love or out of obedience? "I guess I've always thought of the two things as one," she continued. "If one were loving, obedience just naturally followed. And the other way around."

"I don't agree." Shiri was very decided. "At least, I've seen people who were one but not the other."

Ruth sat thinking while she watched Aborakim turn from his father and walk away. Whatever errand he had been sent to carry out, it must be satisfactory to Boaz because she could see a smile on the man's face.

"Look," Shiri whispered. "Boaz and Chalem are coming over here. Do you suppose they mean to speak to us?"

"I hope we haven't done anything wrong," Ruth gasped and got quickly to her feet.

"Here, Father." Chalem's voice was shrill. "Here she is. The woman from Moab."

"Greetings to you, my daughter," Boaz said.

He was tall, Ruth discovered, so tall that she had to tip back her head to meet his eyes. There were not many men who were that tall.

"My lord," she said in a hurried, nervous voice. "Your younger son told me I might glean in your fields. It *is* all right, isn't it?"

"Of course, and also all right that you've come into the shade to rest. Have you been treated kindly?"

"Yes, my lord. I've been befriended by this good woman." Her hand indicated Shiri who stood beside her. "And none of your men have troubled me."

"This wasn't true in the field of Marak, I'm told."

She shot a startled look at him and then glanced down at Chalem. "I told the child nothing, my lord," she protested.

"You didn't need to. Chalem merely told me that Marak was angry. It's easy to guess why."

Chalem looked from his father to Ruth. "What are you talking about?" he demanded. "Would Marak have tried to hurt her because she's a Moabite?"

"Very likely." Boaz' voice was dry. He looked at Ruth again. "Listen, my daughter, you must stay in my fields. You'll be safe here."

Ruth felt such a surge of gratitude and relief that she knew her face must show it.

"I've given notice to the reapers that they're not to molest or insult you," Boaz went on. "Just gather all the grain you want. And your friend, too, of course." He made a small sweep with his hand that took in both Ruth and Shiri.

"See," Chalem cried. "I told you he was generous, didn't I?"

"I hadn't realized how generous," Ruth said.

Boaz gently cuffed his son's head. "You talk too much for someone your age. Go and gather sheaves. You may talk to Ruth later when she's resting. Go now."

The child scampered away and Ruth spoke in astonishment. "My lord, you know my name. How is that?"

Boaz grinned. "Your fame has run before you. Jacob told me about the journey through the wilderness, so I know all about you."

"And I know something of you, too, my lord. Your kindness mended our roof."

"It's nothing," Boaz protested. "I'm happy to help a little." He hesitated and then went on. "I want you to act as though you were one of my own hired workers. Feel free to drink or rest or eat when they do."

For a second she gazed into the kind face above hers and then she sank to the ground in a position of humility and gratitude. "My lord," she said, "why have I found such favor in your sight? You've been wonderfully kind to me even though I'm a foreigner."

Boaz stretched out his hand as though to touch her and then he drew it back. "As I told you, I've heard all about you from Jacob," he said. "How you've given all your devotion and duty to your mother-in-law since your husband died, how you've left your own parents and your own land, even your own god, for the sake of my kinswoman, Naomi."

Ruth looked up, and this time Boaz put out his hand to take hers and lift her to her feet.

"I'm very much impressed by such devotion," he said. "I pray that you'll be fully repaid for all your sacrifice — by the

people here and by our God, Yahweh, under whose wings
you've sought refuge."

"I know He's a mighty God," she admitted, "and able to
do marvelous things."

"He can also be a comfort and a shelter," Boaz said.

For a minute they were silent, staring at each other. They
had said very different things about the Lord God Yahweh,
Ruth realized. She was sure that Boaz was as aware of it as
she was.

"*You* have comforted me, my lord. You have shown as
much kindness to me as though I were your own maidser-
vant. I am more grateful than I can say."

"And I, too, my lord," Shiri said eagerly as though afraid
she might be left out of the generosity Boaz had extended.

"Go in peace," Boaz said to both of the women, but his
gaze came back to Ruth's face. "Glean as long as you like,
drink water whenever you get thirsty and when midday
comes, sit and eat with my servants. You'll be welcome."

If this man were a true reflection of Yahweh, Ruth
thought, then my worship could be as sincere as my belief.
But — and her mind ran back over Marak's lust, Naomi's
occasional bitterness, Aborakim's prejudice, and the coldness of some of the workers in the field. They, too, she was
sure, would claim to be followers of Yahweh and would
believe they reflected Him. So how was she to know
whether or not Boaz was the true reflection? Was it possible
that a man could be better than his God? Oh, surely not —
and yet — certainly some men in Moab were less blood
thirsty than the god, Chemosh.

"Thank you, my lord," she and Shiri said together and
turned to go again to where the reapers swung their stone
toothed scythes in the bright sun, toppling the ripe, heavy
grain to lie in piles of gold along the ground.

At noon, Ruth and Shiri followed the workers toward the
shed. Each of them carried a small loaf of bread, and this,
with the hoped-for water, would constitute their lunch.

"I have a very small jar," Ruth said to Shiri. "My husband was a potter and he made it for me once. As a joke really. It's too small to be much use for anything but it would be perfect here. It would hold just enough water for our meal so that we wouldn't have to keep going over among the workers to ask for something to drink. I'll bring it tomorrow."

Shiri smiled. "That would be wonderful. But even without it, I'm just grateful to be out of the sun and to have the promise of water to drink. You have enough bread?"

"Yes. Naomi was very generous."

They sat in weary silence for a while, chewing on their bread, trying to work up enough courage to walk over to the water jars. Ruth finally looked at Shiri, shrugged and got up to move across the dirt floor.

"Oh, there you are. Do you have food to eat?" The voice was Boaz'.

Ruth was not prepared for the way her heart began to pound. She had been thinking of Boaz as the kindest person she had ever met, but the jolt of her heart made her aware of the fact that he was also an attractive man.

"Yes, my lord." She fought to keep her voice steady and impersonal. "My mother-in-law gave me bread to eat."

Boaz indicated the jar of wine on the ground. "Come and sit here," he insisted. "Don't eat the bread dry. Come and dip it in the wine so that it will be tasty and cool."

For a few seconds she only stood staring. To sit with the owner of the fields, to be asked to dip her bread into his wine was an honor she had never dared consider.

"But my friend, Shiri," she began, indicating the place where Shiri sat across the shed.

"I should have known you'd think of her." Boaz' face was warm with approval. "Bring her, too, then, and come, sit with my reapers."

"My lord," she stammered and knew that her cheeks must show the stain of her pleasure and embarrassment.

"Do come," Chalem called out. "Can she sit beside me, Father? Can I talk to her now?"

"By all means," Boaz agreed. "Call your friend then, my daughter, and sit here with us."

Ruth hurriedly told Shiri of the good fortune that had befallen them, and shyly, they joined the others. The wine was passed, and the bread, dripping with the purple, was cool and tart and refreshing on Ruth's tongue. Perhaps *this* was the result of Naomi's prayers, this acceptance and generosity at the hands of Boaz. Well, whatever had brought her into these particular fields, she could only be grateful.

"Tell me about Moab," Chalem insisted. "Tell me what it's like."

"It's green and fertile," Ruth began, smiling at the little boy. "There are olive and fig trees, rich vineyards, fields of wheat. And little boys help in the fields just as you do."

She went on answering his questions, but suddenly in the middle of one of her descriptions, homesickness took her by the throat so that she almost strangled on the final words. Chalem seemed unaware of anything but his curiosity, but Boaz must have seen the stricken look on her face.

"No more questions, my son. Ruth is weary from the gleaning. Here, my daughter, have some of this roasted grain. It will give you strength for the afternoon's labor."

She smiled, blinking back the sudden tears, taking the rich, nutty smelling, roasted grain from his hands. "Thank you, my lord."

Even after she was full, he pushed more of the grain into her hands. "Take it," he insisted. "You may get hungry as you work."

I can take it to Naomi, she thought. It will make a nice addition to her supper. She put the grain into the little bag that had held the bread. What a lovely feeling to have eaten, to be full and to have more food than she needed.

She looked up to thank Boaz again and her eyes met his. She felt again the shock in her chest as her heart trembled, hesitated and began to race. But she was sure that she saw no reflection of her feeling in Boaz' face.

Shamed, she turned her eyes away. What was the matter

with her that she should react so at her age, in her situation, to a man who was clearly a sort of benefactor and nothing else?

"I must get to work," she said. "Are you coming, Shiri? Thank you again, my lord." She allowed herself one quick glance at Boaz. "I'm grateful to you, my lord, and to your son who rescued me." She smiled at Chalem and hurried away from the shed.

So she did not hear Boaz say to the reapers, "Let her glean as long as she wants and don't scold her or send her away. As my son has already told you, I don't want anyone to insult her."

The reapers nodded agreeably, and Boaz went on with a rush. "As a matter of fact, let grain fall deliberately in the part of the field where she gleans. Don't do it so obviously that she knows what you're doing. I don't want her to feel as though I'm being charitable. I just want her to have all she needs."

The hired men and women nodded again and got up to get back to work. Chalem, delighted with the generosity shown to his new friend, ran after them, but Aborakim, who had been sitting behind Boaz in the shed, turned to his father with an impatient look.

"We have plenty of widows in Bethlehem. You can't feed them all. Why have you chosen a foreigner to be so singled out for such generosity?"

The genial look faded from Boaz' face. "It's not your custom, my son, to question what I do." His voice was cold.

Aborakim flushed. "I only ask out of curiosity, Father. I don't understand, that's all."

"It's not curiosity that brings your questions, but anger. You've made up your mind to hate this woman even though she's never done anything against you. You judge her by her nationality; I judge her by her actions. I happen to think my way is better."

Aborakim stood up. "Forgive me," he said stiffly. "I had no right to speak as I did."

Boaz' voice was a little warmer when he answered. "But you have no intentions of trying to stop hating her?"

"I can't control my heart."

"Nonsense. Of course you can."

Boaz had risen, and they stood staring at each other.

"You've taken a foreigner's part against me," Aborakim stated. "Is it because she is, in your eyes at least, beautiful?"

Boaz stood without moving or speaking, but his gaze never wavered from his son's face. Miserably, Aborakim lowered his eyes at last and swallowed hard.

"I spoke out of turn," the boy said. "I have insulted my father, and I'm ashamed."

"As well you should be. I'm filled with shame myself, that a son of mine would speak so insolently to his father. I don't want to see your face for a while. Please go to work in another of the fields until I'm no longer angry."

"You've never sent me away before."

"You've never deserved it before."

Aborakim turned away, hesitated a second and then spun back toward his father. "If I hated her before," he choked out, "then I hate her twice as much now. She's the first thing to ever come between my father and me."

Before Boaz could answer, the boy had run out of the field and along the dusty path that led to the most distant parts of their land. Boaz stood and watched him go, his face rigid. Then, with a weary shrug of his shoulders, he turned back to the overseeing of his men. But before he began his task, he stood for a few seconds watching Ruth as she bent to pick up the grain. When he looked away, his face had changed. There was still worry and even anger in his eyes, but his mouth had softened into a gentle curve.

17

NAOMI'S FACE was bright with astonishment and pleasure. "I never dreamed you would gather so much," she exclaimed. "Enough for one loaf, perhaps, two at the most. But, look, you've a full ephah of barley. I can't believe it."

Ruth flexed her shoulders. "You wouldn't have any trouble believing it if you could feel the ache in my shoulders. Judging from that, I could believe I'd brought *two* ephahs of barley home." But her eyes were twinkling and her smile was broad.

Naomi was instantly sympathetic. "I can imagine. I'll warm a little oil before we go to bed and rub it into your back and shoulders. I'm sure that will help."

"Thank you, Mother. After a day or two, I'll probably get as used to it as I was to wedging clay. I noticed that the women gathering up sheaves bent almost like dancers while I felt like groaning every time I bent over."

Naomi's attention had gone back to the large amount of grain which Ruth had poured into a wide mouthed jar. "But I still can't get over how much you brought. Did you gather it all in one place, or did you go from field to field?"

"I started out in the field of someone named Marak," Ruth began. "He was, well, very unpleasant, and for a while I was frightened. But I was rescued by a little boy."

"A little boy?" But before Ruth could answer, Naomi indicated the food she was setting out. "Elena gave us a loaf

148

of bread so that the food could be ready when you got home. Tomorrow I'll have time to grind the grain and shape the loaf and bake it myself."

"And tonight I even have some roasted grain for you as a special treat." Ruth took her small bag from her girdle and handed it to her mother-in-law.

Naomi looked at the contents with amazement. "Where did you get this? Surely you didn't steal it? And what do you mean, you were rescued by a small boy?"

Ruth's lighthearted mirth disappeared from her eyes. "What do *you* mean, did I steal it?" Her voice was cool.

Naomi flushed and bit her lip. "I didn't mean anything," she said. "Seeing the bag of roasted grain — I love it more than anything, I think — was such a surprise that I just said the first words —"

"The first words that came into your mind? You've known me intimately for ten years, but do you still think, as most Israelites do, that any Moabite would steal the coins off a dead man's eyes?"

"You're tired," Naomi said. "I didn't mean anything of the kind, and you know it. I don't care where you got the grain. Tell me about the little boy."

The habit of obedience and acquiescence was strong. Ruth shoved her momentary anger into the back of her mind. What did she expect anyhow? Sensitive understanding from an Israelite?

The sudden, shamed recognition of her own prejudice, matching Naomi's in its generalization, came with a shock. She was, in this area, really no better than anyone else.

"It was Chalem, the son of Boaz," she began, softening her voice. "He has no idea, even yet, that he rescued me, but he did."

She recounted the events that had taken place in the field of Marak and saw the anger and dismay on Naomi's face.

"Marak had no right," Naomi declared. "No right at all."

"No moral right, Mother, but he was in a position I couldn't quarrel with."

"I knew it. I knew it." Naomi muttered as she beckoned

Ruth to the mat in the middle of the floor. "No decent woman should have to go out with those rough field hands. Surely *he* didn't give you the grain?"

Ruth sat down wearily and looked longingly at the food. She hoped Naomi's prayer of blessing would be brief. "No, Boaz gave it to me."

"Boaz?"

Ruth nodded. "I'll tell you all about it," she began, but Naomi interrupted.

"Wait until I pray. Then you can eat while you talk.

"Thank you, Lord God, for bringing my daughter home safely. Thank you for filling her hands with food. Fill our hearts with love and forgiveness. Amen."

For a few seconds their eyes met. Ruth recognized that the prayer had held apology, and she accepted it.

"Here, Mother," she said. "Have the roasted grain. I had plenty at noon. Wait until I tell you what happened."

The story poured out between bites of food, and Naomi's reaction was as awed and appreciative as Ruth had wanted.

"I can't believe that you went to the fields of Boaz, that Chalem actually invited you. Boaz is one of my husband's closest kinsmen. And he knew who you were, you say?"

Ruth swallowed a bite of cheese. "He seemed to know all about me. He'd heard about me from Jacob, he said."

"That's wonderful. Now you do as he says. You stay in his fields and stay close to his reapers. That way, nothing will happen to you. And if he continues to be as generous as he was today, we'll soon have enough grain to see us through many months. I can't tell you how pleased I am."

"I was just lucky," Ruth said, remembering the charms Chemosh's followers in Moab wore to bring good luck.

Naomi's answer was sharp. "Don't be silly. Luck had nothing to do with it. I prayed that the Lord would protect you, and He did. Blessed is the name of Yahweh."

Ruth woke, as was her custom, when dawn began to filter its first gray light through the cracks between the

edges of the door opening and the skin that hung over it.
Moving cautiously so that she wouldn't wake her mother-
in-law, she rolled onto her back, feeling a stabbing ache in
the muscles across her shoulders. She wondered if the
stooping would ever become easy and graceful for her.
Probably not, she thought ruefully.

This private time of waking was usually the only time
during the day when she was free to pursue her own
thoughts, to let her mind wander achingly over the past or
timidly into the future. It was the only time she let herself
remember Mahlon, the feel of his arms and his lips, the
roughness of his beard against her cheek.

Sometimes she dreamed about him, and in the quiet
dawn, she would cherish the dream, reliving the vividness
of touch and voice. Last night, she had dreamed of laughter
and joy, of walking in the sunlight as though she were a
child again, with her hand in a large, warm masculine
hand. Just so had she often dreamed of Mahlon, even when
he was still living.

An unexpected shock of recognition slowed her circling
thoughts. It hadn't been Mahlon walking beside her, holding her hand. It had been Boaz.

This was foolish, she told herself. Foolish and wicked.
She had been offered friendship and kindness, and her silly
tendency to dream had made her as giddy as an adolescent
girl.

Gradually her thoughts slid from shame to reality. She
couldn't just lie here recalling dreams. There was work to be
done and no one but her to do it. Reaching for her sandals,
she sat up and began to get ready for the coming day.

The time of harvest slid slowly by. To her astonishment,
Ruth found that she did acquire some of the ease of the
practiced gatherers of grain. She learned to stoop with a
fluid grace, to pick up the fallen grain so gently that the
ripened heads were never lost.

For several days, Shiri worked beside her, but one morning she did not appear. Ruth looked for her, wondering if she were ill or had moved to another field, but there was no one she could ask.

During the noon rest, Chalem came up to Ruth with great excitement.

"I heard something about your friend," he announced.

"My friend?"

"Yes, the woman who gleaned beside you. I thought you'd like to know what happened."

"She's not hurt or ill?" Ruth could not keep the anxious note out of her voice.

"No, she's going to be married." Chalem's eyes sparkled with the delight of his announcement.

"Married?"

"I saw the whole thing," Chalem confided. "I had gone into the village on an errand for my father, and coming back, I saw such a group of men at the gate that I stopped to see what was going on."

Ruth patted the ground beside her, and the child sat down, cross legged, in the dirt. "They had all left the fields because a decision had to be made before a certain man left town. They were all dirty and hot from working, but they were laughing, too, and acting as though they were having a good time."

"But what has all this to do with Shiri?"

"I *thought* that was her name," Chalem said with satisfaction. "So when I heard them talking about her, I listened. One of the men — the one who was leaving town — said he would be her go'el. Doesn't that mean husband?"

"Not always but sometimes it does."

"Well, anyhow, one man took off his sandal and gave it to another, and there was a lot of shouting. One of the boys told me that the one shouting the loudest was her father-in-law. In relief, guess. It isn't easy to marry off a widow." He looked very wise and knowing.

"No, it isn't," she agreed. "But that's lovely for Shiri. No wonder she didn't come to glean. She probably left town with the man who will be her go'el. He'll take care of her now."

Chalem looked up at her shyly under the long fringe of his dark eyelashes. "If I were older, I'd take care of *you*," he said in a rush.

She wanted to hug him, but she wouldn't hurt his dignity.

"Thank you, my lord," she said, getting up. "If you were older, I would be very happy. As it is, you've made me proud."

His cheeks were red as he jumped to his feet. "Don't tell Aborakim," he warned her.

"Don't tell Aborakim what?"

Startled, Ruth looked up to see that young man staring at his little brother.

Chalem, flustered, groped for words, and Ruth, touched with pity for the small boy, spoke up. "He didn't want you to know that he had spent his noon hour asking questions about Moab."

"A stupid waste of time." Aborakim bit off the words. "I could think of a dozen better ways for him to use his time."

"Learning is never truly a waste of time, my lord." A stubborn note crept into Ruth's voice.

"Learning about foolish things is. Learning about our own history would be a far greater advantage. He probably doesn't even know the story of Moses in the wilderness."

The insult was so obvious that even Ruth winced. But to her delight, Chalem did not fly into a fit of temper and denial. He looked up at his big brother and spoke in a voice that was almost silky.

"And if I don't know the story, it's probably the fault of the teacher. I think you're the one who told it to me."

Aborakim stared and then whirled toward Ruth. "Is there some kind of witchcraft in you that you turn everyone against me? First my father and now my brother. I wish I'd never seen your face."

Chalem gasped and stood watching Aborakim stride

away from them. "He has no right to talk like that," he cried. "I'll — I'll tell him —"

But Ruth's hand caught the boy's thin arm and held him fast. "Let him go," she said. "It's not important. Truly it isn't."

But in her heart she knew that it was terribly important. What had Aborakim meant when he said, "First my father...?"

Chalem glanced up at her in embarrassment. "Thank you for not telling him what I *really* said to you."

She smiled. If she had been able to have a child early in her marriage, he would be nearly the age of this boy. "Why should I have to share the nicest thing that has been said to me since I came to Bethlehem?" she asked and was rewarded with a brilliant smile.

Someone called Chalem's name, and with a quick wave, he was gone. Ruth left the shed to go back to her gleaning, her head whirling with a hundred thoughts. It was wonderful for Shiri, of course, that the cousin — she had said it was a cousin, hadn't she? — was willing to take her as his wife and responsibility. "I hope he's not married," Ruth said to herself. "I wouldn't want his wife to feel as I once felt."

But after only a short time her thoughts centered on the sons of Boaz. She had hoped only that the people of Bethlehem would accept her, and here were two boys who, under ordinary circumstances, would hardly be aware of her, and yet one of them hated her and the other almost loved her.

And their father, Ruth thought, stooping for the fallen grain. How does their father feel? Does his generosity simply stem from pity or a feeling of responsibility toward Naomi?

Why should it matter to me, she asked herself fiercely.

There was no ready answer. She only knew that in some strange way it did matter. It mattered very much.

18

RUTH AND NAOMI sat outside their door, eating breakfast in the shade of the fig tree. Summer was so close that
the dampness of winter and the sweet freshness of early
spring were almost forgotten. As soon as the sun slid up
over the edge of the world, the heat was intense. It was
nothing like the breathless oppression that had filled the
valley of the Dead Sea. Rather, it was a dry, light heat that
made rocks too hot to touch and dried perspiration almost
before it could form. But the house was no longer pleasant,
except at night, and so they spent as much time as possible
outside.

"If you feel yourself getting light-headed or dizzy,"
Naomi cautioned, "go into the shade of the shed. Field
workers often suffer sunstroke this time of year. You know
that."

"If I were younger," Ruth said, smiling to show she
wasn't wholly serious, "I'd be far more concerned about
sunburn than sunstroke. Already, my face and arms are
getting dark. I look like a servant."

"You're not too dark yet." Naomi's eyes were critical. "So
far, you've only turned a sort of gold color. I suppose if the
harvest lasts too much longer, you'll begin to get brown. I
know you'd hate that."

"Well, the barley harvest has ended and we're beginning
to harvest the wheat, so it won't be much longer, I guess."

"And we'll be fixed for months," Naomi said with satisfaction. "You've gleaned enough in Boaz' fields to make me feel as though we were almost rich."

"Have you given any further thought to selling your husband's fields?" Ruth asked.

"I've thought of it often. And I've inquired about what can be done. My nephew says that it must be sold to someone in my lord's family. The closest kinsman possible. I'd like to offer it to Boaz, out of gratitude for all he's done for us, but he's not the nearest kinsman."

Ruth's eyes flew to Naomi's face. "Not the nearest kinsman?" she asked in a whisper.

Naomi was intent on the bowl of milk she was lifting to her lips. "No. Joamech is."

Ruth was aware of a great sense of grief which was so unexpected that she had no defense against it.

Ruth had to wet her lips with her tongue before she could ask her question. "Joamech? I don't know him, do I?"

"Probably not." Naomi's voice was casual. "He and his wife and their children — three or four of them — live on the other side of town. He's a potter, too, as Elimelech was."

Ruth bent her head and stared, sightlessly, at the ground. She didn't have to ask herself why her heart was fluttering like a wounded bird. She knew why. Without ever formulating her desire into words, or even dreams, she had let the idea of Boaz' relationship to Elimelech be a hope and a promise. When the harvest was over, when life was calmer again, maybe Naomi would realize that Ruth was still young enough to marry, to bear sons. And she would realize that Boaz was a widower and a kinsman, and since the Israelites had this custom of marriage to a husband's kinsman, why maybe — just maybe —

Her mind stumbled to a halt, confused and reluctant to go on any further. She had not, until Naomi's casual remark, even realized that such thoughts had been forming in her heart.

Naomi looked up, her mouth ringed with milk as a child's mouth would be. "What is it?" she said. "You look pale. Are you ill?"

Ruth did not meet her mother-in-law's eyes. "No," she said in a dry, husky voice. "No. I must hurry or I'll be late in the fields. May I leave without helping you clear the breakfast things?"

"Of course. Don't forget the basket. Your shawl is being ruined by the grain. Better that you use the basket. And there's enough room in it to carry your little water jar."

"They may think me greedy to carry a basket."

"Nonsense!" Naomi was very hearty and practical. "Boaz has given you so much grain every day that a basket only makes sense. Go along now. I'll have food ready when you come home. Do you have something for your noontime food?"

"Yes. I have a small loaf. And Boaz —" Her voice trembled a little on the name, but Naomi didn't seem to notice. "Boaz always gives me some roasted grain or a bit of cheese. He's — he's very kind."

For a few seconds, Ruth let her eyes look into Naomi's face. She wanted to cry out, "Oh, listen to what I'm saying! Look at me and *see* me." But of course she didn't say it. Naomi would stare at her in honest bewilderment, wondering what she meant.

"I'm going now, Mother," Ruth mumbled.

"Yahweh go with you." But Naomi's words came more from habit than concern.

"And Yahweh be with you, too," Ruth returned, but her words came more from duty than conviction.

Picking up the basket, Ruth turned and started across the field. The houses of Bethlehem, clustered together, were behind her, but she always stopped on the edge of the first rise to look back at them. The almost level rays of the climbing sun threw the whitewashed buildings into sharp, angled relief, so that the town always looked like something that might have been made by an artisan. Some giant potter, Ruth's fancy had suggested, who could make square pots instead of round ones and who could pile them most beautifully in the early light.

Out of habit, she stopped to look back. But today there

was no joy in it for her. For the first time she recognized with honesty that she had looked back, not just because the shapes of the houses were pleasing to her, but because from that spot she could see the house of Boaz. The largest and richest house in the village, it raised its second story above the other, smaller houses to form a sort of landmark against the sky.

Was I thinking of it as *my* house, Ruth wondered. Had I dared to believe, to hope that Naomi would go to Boaz with the same proposition she had made to Mahlon about Orpah?

She remembered Chalem's eager announcement of the finding of a go'el for Shiri. Was I hoping for the same thing for me, Ruth thought. Oh, surely not. I wouldn't dare reach so high, would I?

She walked slowly along the dusty path that led to the field where Boaz' servants were cutting and reaping the wheat.

Joamech, she thought. A man with a wife and four children. Would Naomi go to him and offer him the land? And if she did, would she offer him her daughter-in-law, too? Even if the man is better than most men, Ruth thought in anguish, he's already married. *I don't want to be a second wife in Joamech's house.*

I could never be like Patima, Ruth thought, and just accept something because it was the thing to do. She remembered, as she remembered in all the darkest moments of her life, the day Patima's baby had been offered as a burnt offering to Chemosh. She recalled the ravaged grief on Patima's face that eventually smoothed itself out into acceptance. But there had been no acceptance in the young Ruth who had stood with her arms hugging her own barren body, weeping with agony at the waste of new life. Now in the early morning, she wept again at the bitterness of her memory and at the death Naomi had unknowingly dealt to Ruth's young dream.

Just at that moment, a voice cut through her absorption. "Are you weeping, my daughter? Can I help you?"

Boaz stood a few feet away from her on the path. Would she never outgrow this tendency to go so deeply within herself that she was totally unaware of things around her?

She jumped, startled. "My lord," she said and was instantly aware of the wetness on her cheeks, drying in the morning air. "It's nothing, my lord."

Boaz looked worried. "Are you sure you're all right?"

When she nodded, he asked, "Are you heading for my fields?"

"Yes, my lord. If you still grant me permission."

"Of course. Come, I'll walk along with you."

It was an unheard of situation. She could only think that perhaps he wanted to give her further instructions or to caution her against some danger.

"Yes, my lord." Furtively, she scrubbed the last of the tears from her face.

"Your weeping," Boaz said, "it troubles me. Is there a special problem in your life, or do you still grieve for your husband and your home?"

The habitual proper answer trembled on her lips. "It's nothing, my lord," she planned to say, but when she looked up to say the words, Boaz' eyes met hers. His face was not merely polite. It was warm with caring.

"I've been very foolish, my lord," Ruth said, the words tumbling out without pretense. "I was crying over something that happened many years ago and over something that happened this morning. I was admitting to myself that I've been foolish, and this is never very pleasant."

He nodded. "I know. I've had to admit my failings, too."

She was shocked. Men didn't say things like that. At least not any man she had ever known.

"You, my lord?"

"Of course me. It's very hard to admit such failure to myself, harder still to admit it to Yahweh. Impossible to admit it to my sons."

He was smiling, but she knew he was not teasing.

"To Yahweh, my lord? You admit such things to your God?"

"Naturally. To confess my sin, to ask for His forgiveness and mercy is a large part of our belief. Don't you understand that?"

"It never occurred to me that He would listen to me, my lord."

There! She had said it. Not to Naomi who would never have been able to understand, but to the man who had given her food and a sense of dignity.

Boaz stopped and stared at her. "But you believe in Him?"

"Yes, my lord. But I've never — I've never been able to admit my needs to anyone."

"Not to your husband?"

"No, my lord." Unexpectedly, the words rushed out. "It wasn't his fault, my lord. If I had asked him to, he might have listened. I'm too proud, my lord. I feel that my thoughts are not like anyone else's."

She stood stricken, unable to believe she had said these words. It was true that Mahlon was not a talker, but it was equally true that she had never had the courage to risk a confidence. Why had she taken the risk now? And with a stranger.

But Boaz only nodded. "The sin of pride," he murmured. "It's the most subtle sin of all. For example, every morning when I come across to the fields, I stop to admire the light and shadow on the town. At least that's what I tell myself. I wonder if I'm not admiring the sight of my own house."

"But the light and shadow *are* beautiful, my lord," she said, her voice breathless. "There, at the edge of that field, the sun shines on the buildings in such a way as to make them look — look as though —" Her words faltered and stopped.

"You turn and look back, too," he said.

"Yes, my lord."

For a long moment, Boaz merely stared at her and then he looked away. "I've pointed it out to Aborakim," he said lightly. "I've told him it looks like a painting on an Egyptian pot I'd seen once. He laughs at me. But Chalem — Chalem sees it, too. He wants to be a potter, you know."

"No, my lord, I didn't know." She was having trouble forming the words because her heart was beating high in her throat and almost strangling her."

"I wish Elimelech were still living," Boaz said in that same light voice, "then he could teach the lad. Well, Joamech might be willing to take the boy as an apprentice. He has only one son to carry on the trade. He might welcome another boy."

"Yes, my lord." But her mind was whirling.

"He's a kinsman,' Boaz went on. "To both your father-in-law and to me."

"Yes, I know." Her voice was faint. "My mother-in-law was speaking of him only this morning."

Boaz was silent. When he finally spoke, his voice was thoughtful. "Yes, well, I suppose she would be thinking of him. He's your nearest kinsman."

Just at that moment, they came to a fork in the path. The path to the left wound slowly and somewhat laboriously across the hills that edged the fields of Boaz, while the right hand one dropped directly, if precipitously, through a narrow pass to the closest fields.

Boaz waved his hand toward the right path. "Have you been warned about the danger of going this way?"

She was eager to talk of anything that would take her mind away from the depressing subject of Joamech. "Yes, my mother-in-law warned me about it when I first started to go out to glean. And Shiri, the woman who was so friendly to me before she left to get married, told me always to take the longer path."

"And do you?" He was smiling at her, and she smiled back.

"It's a temptation not to," she confessed. "The one path so direct and short, the other so much longer. But I almost always do as I've been told."

"*Almost* always?"

"Once or twice," she admitted, "when I've been late, I've taken the steeper path. I've always been very careful."

"Careful is not enough." He was as stern as though she were a child. "That steep path is curiously slippery. The clay is slick even in the driest seasons. I'd rather you didn't go that way. Ever."

She knew, without his having to say it, that his sternness stemmed from concern. "Yes, my lord," she said.

"It's a great worry to me," Boaz muttered, starting up the other path. "Aborakim *will* come this way, whether or not I want it, and I worry that Chalem may start the habit. The path is not only slippery, but some people speak of seeing a wolf in the vicinity. It's unusual for wolves to come quite so close to the fields where men are working, though they're a constant threat to shepherds. Of course, I'm not sure there's even a wolf around here, but there's no need to take chances."

"I'll get an earlier start each day," she promised fervently, walking closely behind him and glancing over her shoulder. "Then I won't be tempted to use the short path."

"It would be one less thing to worry about," he said with a quick glance back at her.

They walked in silence, Ruth content with the fact that they were together. Her mind kept replaying parts of their conversation, and she wondered again that she, the reticient one, should have spoken with such candor.

A voice called out in greeting. "My lord."

Ruth, looking up, saw that they had reached the first field.

Boaz raised his hand in greeting. "May the Lord be with you," he cried. Then he turned to Ruth. "Remember, my daughter, that there's always someone willing to listen to you. But you have to be willing to speak."

"Yes, my lord."

"Then go in the peace of Yahweh," he said and turned away from her.

"Mother," Ruth said. She and Naomi had just lain down on their sleeping mats. "Mother, may I speak to you?"

"Of course." In the dim light of the small lamp, Naomi peered over towards Ruth.

But I just can't tell her what I meant to, Ruth realized. I can't say that I want her to ask Boaz to be a go'el for me. No matter what Boaz said about people being willing to listen, I can't say it.

"I only wondered," Ruth finally said, "I only wondered if you thought Yahweh heard the prayers of everyone. I mean everyone who believed in Him. Could I pray to Him?" she blurted out.

Naomi sat up. "You mean you haven't been?"

"A little," Ruth confessed. "I've thanked Him for some things. But I've never dared ask for anything."

"If I hadn't asked," Naomi said reasonably, "would I be here now?"

"No, but you, well, you were born among Yahweh's people."

"But you believe," Naomi argued. "Maybe you don't understand much of the law or know Yahweh as fully as we do, but He will surely listen."

"It wouldn't be too bold of me?"

"Of course not. Just ask Him for strength and protection," Naomi instructed. "You can ask Him for anything you need."

"Or want?" Ruth's voice was small.

"Of course. Within reason. Remember how I asked and how my prayer was answered?"

"Well," Ruth conceded, "I'll try."

Naomi lay down again and the shed became very still.

But how do I begin, Ruth thought. How do I admit even to Yahweh that what I want is something no woman should ask for? How would I dare ask for a go'el when I wasn't willing to share Mahlon with Orpah?

The unexpectedness of her next thought hit her like a blow. How could she dream of becoming the wife of Boaz when his older son hated her? Even if Boaz found her fair, he would surely not antagonize his son by taking a foreigner for a wife.

19

AT THE SAME TIME that Ruth was struggling with her feelings of guilt and frustration, Chalem was having his own struggle with guilt and pride. His father had forbidden him to eat any of the figs until they were fully ripe, but the temptation had been too great to resist. Now, some hours after he had eaten the forbidden fruit, Chalem was suffering the consequences of his sin. Even Adam and Eve, he thought dolefully, could not have known such quick and devastating punishment in the Garden.

A little alarmed that his thoughts might be blasphemous, Chalem looked uneasily about his dimly lit room as he clutched his stomach. If he went to his father for help, he would have to admit he had disobeyed, and, to compound his misery, he'd have to admit he was still a child who needed assistance and not a man who could handle his own problems.

For a long time, he twisted miserably on his sleeping mat, wishing he had listened to his father. He thought, achingly, of his mother and of the comfort of her cool hands on his face when he had been ill. Finally, swallowing his pride, he got up and went to his father's room.

"Abba." The intimate, childish word for father came out before he could repress it.

Boaz turned so quickly that Chalem was sure he, too, had been awake.

"What is it?"

"I'm — I'm sick. There are a thousand evil spirits struggling in my belly."

Boaz smiled. "Only a thousand, my son?"

Chalem's pride deserted him entirely, and with no thought at all for his forced admission of guilt, he dropped to his knees beside his father. "Oh, please, Abba, I ate the figs and I'm dying."

"I've never known a boy to die from eating unripe figs," Boaz stated, "but then, of course, I don't know how many you ate."

"Only a few." Chalem didn't even try to hold back the tears. "Only a few, Abba. It can't be just the figs. It must be the evil spirits."

"Probably." Boaz' tone was dry. "Well, come then. If there's any fire left, I'll heat some water and brew a hot drink of mint and cumin."

Chalem groaned. "It will scald my insides."

"No doubt. But it will scald the evil spirits, too. Or cause you to get rid of the figs."

By the time Chalem's pain had been eased, both he and his father were a long way from sleep.

"I'll never disobey you again," Chalem promised, white and shaking.

"I'm sure you won't. At least, you won't until the green grapes begin to get plump and slightly blue, and you won't be able to wait until harvest."

Chalem gave a sickly grin. They walked together back to Boaz' room, and the boy stood hesitating in the doorway.

"I'm sorry, Father," he said, "that I had to make you get up. I know it's not a man's work to fix hot drinks. I'm sorry I made it necessary."

Boaz smiled and patted his sleeping mat with invitation. "And I know you would have found more comfort in a mother's care, my boy. A father has no training in being gentle."

In response to the invitation, Chalem sat cross-legged on the mat and watched with satisfaction as his father sat beside him. "You're more gentle than most fathers," Chalem said.

"Of course you don't know many fathers that well," Boaz said, his eyes twinkling.

"The boys talk," Chalem confided. "Sometimes I have to lie a little and say you beat me. It's embarrassing to be the only boy whose father never uses a rod."

"I could learn if it's necessary."

Chalem only smiled and shook his head. The pain was all gone but he felt light and wobbly and he had no desire to leave the quiet comfort of his father's room.

Boaz yawned and lay down on his mat. "Here," he instructed, "lie down here on this rug. If the pain comes again you won't have to walk in the dark."

With a sigh, Chalem did as he was told. After a minute or two of silence, the boy spoke abruptly.

"Father," he said, "do you think anyone in Bethlehem would be a go'el for Ruth?"

Boaz made a startled movement. "What made you think of that?" he asked, his voice shaken. "How did you know —" He stopped as though he had swallowed the words.

"How I did I know what?"

"Nothing. Nothing at all. What made you ask the question?"

"Because Shiri's father-in-law found a go'el for her, and Ruth acted as though that was something wonderful. So I just thought, well, I wish someone would be a go'el for her. I'm too young."

The last three words were barely a whisper, but Boaz heard them, and a look of amusement and then compassion crossed his face.

"A go'el must be a relative," Boaz said.

"I know that, but aren't *we* kinsmen? Aborakim said we were."

"*Aborakim* said that?"

"He didn't sound happy about it," Chalem admitted. "He was telling me to stay away from her. 'Isn't it bad enough that we have to be related to her?' he said."

All at once, Chalem's eyes grew very wide and his mouth formed a circle of amazement. For a few seconds he was unable to say the words that he wanted to say, but finally he stuttered, "You could do it. You could be her go'el."

"Aren't you a little young to be a matchmaker?"

He might be young to be a matchmaker, Chalem thought, but he was old enough to recognize the fact that his suggestion was not as startling to his father as he had supposed it would be.

"Couldn't you be her go'el?" Chalem begged.

"I'm at least fifteen years older than she is," Boaz began, but the boy diminished the importance of that with a disdainful snort.

"She's old enough to be my mother," he argued. "She told me if she'd had a child when she was first married, he'd be almost as old as I am."

Father and son were silent, looking at each other. "When did she tell you that?" Boaz asked.

"One time." Chalem was vague. He was thinking of something else, something he had never thought of before.

"If you were her go'el," he said in a tone of discovery, "she would be a sort of mother to me, wouldn't she?"

"I suppose she would. But you're not being reasonable. Not only am I too old for her, but I'm not the nearest kinsman."

"You're not?" The two small words held a weight of tragedy.

"No, I'm not. Joamech is."

"Joamech?"

"Yes. The very person you want most to please. If there is any chance of your learning the pottery trade, Joamech will have to be your master. How do you think he'd feel if we cheated him out of his rightful heritage?"

"Ruth is a heritage?"

"Well, not so much Ruth herself. But Ruth's father-in-law owned land, and I'm sure it will be sold to the man who will be her go'el. Then Ruth can raise up sons to her dead husband's name, and they can inherit the land."

Chalem gazed at his father in despair. "Can't you change the law? She's so beautiful and so good."

Boaz shook his head. "I'm aware that she's beautiful and good, but the law is the law."

Chalem rolled away from his father and his voice was muffled when he spoke. "I'll pray about it," he declared. "I'll ask Yahweh to let us have her."

"And what about Aborakim?" But there was no hint of teasing in Boaz' voice. It was as though he really wanted to know. "You know how he feels about her."

"If Yahweh gives her to us," Chalem said, "then I'm not going to worry about Aborakim. I'll figure out something."

Boaz hesitated a minute and then he put a gentle hand on his son's arm. "Then, may Yahweh hear your prayer," he whispered in so soft a voice Chalem did not hear. "Now go to sleep."

But it was a long time before Boaz could follow the advice he gave his son.

It was still dark when Ruth woke up. For a minute she lay in silence, wondering if it was the approach of dawn which had ended her sleep. But she heard none of the sounds of morning; no birds sang to welcome the growing light. Something must have disturbed her sleep, something unusual.

For a few seconds, she felt a touch of fear, but she pushed the sensation aside. She could not afford to tremble like a child each time her sleep was broken.

Then she heard the sound that must be a replica of the sound that had wakened her. A high, breaking cry of pain. Ruth raised her head, startled, and almost immediately knew what it was. Altah must be in the final stages of her labor. She had looked weary the past several days and had confessed to Naomi that her back ached and that her time must be near.

In less than a minute there was still another cry, harsh and drawn out and then sliced off by a thin, high, new sound. The baby was here. The baby was born.

Ruth shifted her position, realizing for the first time that she had been holding herself rigid and taut, as though by her own straining muscles she could help Altah. So had it been when Patima or Orpah had given birth, and each time, some part of Ruth had rejoiced over the sound of the baby's wail. But an equal part of her had wept with desolation that the child had been born to someone else.

Now, she was feeling something different. She had fallen asleep the night before, unable to pray to Yahweh, unable to shape her desires and her needs into words, so sure had she been of Yahweh's rejection.

But Altah's child's cry was like a clear, sweet sound of hope. Ruth felt no envy, no anger, only joy that Altah had been safely delivered.

The words of prayer came without any feeling of restraint or caution. "Oh, Yahweh, Lord, of Israel," she whispered, not even caring that Naomi might wake, "thank you for keeping Altah safe. Be with her and with her child."

A sensation of quiet warmth spread through Ruth's body. She had a quick memory of the time she had fallen and hurt herself, and her father, gentle for once, had picked her up and cradled her against his chest. It had been the one time in her life when she had felt cherished and safe, and now she was feeling that way again.

"Oh, Yahweh, my God," she went on in a whisper. "Hear me — though I am only a Moabite, only a widow. You've got to hear me, Lord, because I need you — and there's no one else. If Boaz can't or won't redeem me, then just let me remain a widow. Please, Lord, I don't want to marry a man who already has a wife. Oh, Lord, please!"

So intent was she on her prayer that she did not hear the change in Naomi's breathing or the shifting of her body on the mat. Ruth heard only the pounding of her own heart, she was aware only of the spirit of peace and love which filled her.

This, she thought gratefully, is what I was trying to explain to Naomi when I was talking about the difference between belief and faith. I've believed in Yahweh ever since the caravan came though Bezer, but it's only now, in this moment of honest prayer, that I have come even close to having faith. Not only faith that Yahweh is a mighty God but also that He cares about *me*, that my wants and needs are known to Him and that He will listen to me. He is listening to me right now!

The feeling of warm security held her with such a sense of reality that it was as though the mat on which she was lying had suddenly become a pair of arms. For the few minutes of awareness before she slept again, she had absolutely no doubt that Yahweh had stooped to listen and to hold her in His arms.

Sleep engulfed Ruth so quickly that she was aware of nothing more until dawn. She did not hear Naomi's twisting and turning, the faint sound of her weeping or the sibilant whisper of her prayers that begged for the wisdom that was needed to shape a plan.

In the morning on her way to the fields, Ruth stopped at the house where Altah and Jacob lived. Even before she entered the door, she was aware of the smell of warmed oil and the sound of happy voices.

"Good morning." Ruth stood shyly just inside the door and smiled toward Altah's cousin, who returned the smile. "Did I hear the sound of a child in the night? Altah's child?"

"You did indeed. A fine son. Wait, I'll get him so you can see him."

"Give Altah my love, my best wishes. Tell her I'm happy for her."

The girl nodded and ducked under a low door. In only a few seconds, she was back, a small bundle in her arms.

Ruth pulled away the covers and gazed down into the tiny puckered face. Gently she touched her finger to the dark hair that grew so thickly on the little round head. "And Altah," she asked at last. "Is she all right?"

"She's fine. In seven days she'll be out of seclusion and you can see her. She got along very well for a first baby. The midwife said it was as though she had help."

Ruth remembered the tension of her own body and of the overwhelming sense of Yahweh's presence. "And I'm sure she did," Ruth said. "Everyone who loved her was praying for her, and surely Yahweh hears such prayers and is merciful."

The girl looked down at the baby in her arms and then up at Ruth. "It's hard to remember you're a Moabite," she blurted out, "when you talk like one of us."

"I want to be one of you," Ruth said slowly. "If you think of me that way, then I'm grateful."

She touched the baby's head again and then turned to hurry out the door. But all the way to the fields, she carried the memory of the child's face — the feathery brows bent in a scowl of concentration, the mouth pursed as though to take nourishment from the air itself.

For the first time in years, she did not feel the ache of her own barrenness. It was enough that a child had been safely born.

When she got to the fields, she found the harvesters making plans for the beginning of the barley threshing. The grain was dry enough, they declared, and the evening breeze from the west was lively and brisk. They would work only until midafternoon, Ruth was told, and then they would rest for an hour or so before they went to the threshing floor to begin the work there.

The rest was necessary because the work would last until dark. "In fact," one of the men called out, "the celebrating lasts until well after dark — or I hope it will. If Boaz is as generous as he usually is at threshing time, we'll do more drinking than working."

"It may be a celebration for the men," one of the women whispered to Ruth, "but it means nothing to the gleaners except a shorter day in the field and less grain gathered up. Women don't go near the threshing floor."

"It was the same in Moab," Ruth agreed. "The only women who went near the threshers were women who—" She faltered, seeking the right word.

"I know. We have women like that, too. Well, at least the

evenings are cool and breezy, and we can get some extra rest during the threshing days."

Ruth turned without further conversation to the task of gleaning. Her body was completely adapted to the work, she realized, and there was no fatigue in her at all. She felt only regret that the day in the fields would be shortened, so much had she come to cherish being close enough to Boaz to hear his voice or even, on occasion, to meet his eyes and see him smile.

part IV

Then Naomi...said to her, "My daughter, shall I not seek security for you, that it may be well with you?"...So [Ruth] went down to the threshing floor and did according to all that her mother-in-law had commanded her.... So Boaz took Ruth, and she became his wife.

Ruth 3:1,6; 4:13*a*

20

THAT AFTERNOON, Ruth came home early from the fields to find Naomi crouched over the quern, grinding grain. The older woman looked up in astonishment.

"Why are you home early? Is the harvest completely finished?"

"No, not completely." Ruth put down the bundle of grain she was carrying and then stretched her arms over her head in a gesture of relief. "But the threshing starts tonight. So the men were given a few hours to rest. Naturally, we can't glean if they're not harvesting."

"Threshing? So soon?"

"The barley. It's dry enough by now, and the men say that the evening breeze is finally brisk enough to make the winnowing possible." Ruth stood looking down at Naomi. "Let me do that, Mother."

Naomi sat back on her heels and squinted up at Ruth. "Nonsense. I'm perfectly able to do it, and you've been working hard enough."

Ruth looked around with a helpless feeling. "I don't know what to do," she confessed. "I've become so used to the fields that it feels odd to be at home."

"You manage well enough on the Sabbath," Naomi retorted. "It wouldn't hurt to take a couple of hours now and rest. Why don't you pull your mat out into the shade and lie down?"

Ruth smiled. "I don't know. I feel as though the heavens

might fall down if I took a nap in the middle of an ordinary
day."

"We'll risk it," Naomi returned dryly. "Go on now. It's
almost pleasant here in this shade. I know. I've reached the
point where it's going to take a lot to tempt me away from
this fig tree. Lie down and rest, but don't be alarmed if you
wake up and I'm gone. I've promised Elena that I'd come by
for a few minutes."

"If you're sure," Ruth began.

"I'm sure," Naomi answered.

Ruth did as she was told, stretching out on the mat.

"Sleep in peace, my daughter," Naomi said.

"Thank you, Mother," Ruth grinned before she turned
away. "I feel as though I were a princess — or the mother of
a king — lying down so luxuriously in the middle of the
day."

"Who knows?" Naomi's words were light and un-
planned. "Someday you may be the mother of a king. Or
the grandmother."

They both smiled to show that the words meant nothing.
But when Ruth had turned over to pillow her cheek against
her arm, Naomi's face was bright with sudden excitement.

Chalem had been trying to sleep so that he might be able
to stay awake for the threshing festivities, but his eyes
would not close. His thoughts skittered and skipped from
one place to another. He was remembering the middle-of-
the-night conversation with his father and his own declaration to pray for a miracle. The trouble was that he had fallen
asleep in the middle of his first few words. And he was a
little afraid to pray now, since he was supposed to be
sleeping, and he wasn't at all sure that his father's God
would listen to a small boy who was being disobedient
again.

He finally decided he could not lie still another minute,
so he got up off his mat and slipped quietly outside. He
could rest just as well taking a walk, he told himself, as
lying on his mat.

He had gone only a short distance when he noticed a woman coming toward him. At first, he wasn't sure who it was, but when he got closer he recognized Ruth's mother-in-law. He had never spoken to her, but he had seen her with the other village women, and Aborakim had told him who she was.

"Peace," he said shyly when he got closer to her. "May the peace of Yahweh be with you."

"And with you, too, my son." Naomi's smile was warm.

Chalem hesitated and then blurted out, "You're Ruth's mother-in-law, aren't you?"

"Yes. And you're the son of Boaz. I think Ruth said your name is Chalem."

"She's talked about me?" he said with pleasure.

"Indeed. Many times. Your friendship has meant a great deal to her."

He nodded solemnly. "It's not easy for a foreigner in a strange land."

"As well I know. I was a foreigner for a long time when I was in Moab."

The thought was a new one to Chalem. "I never thought about *us* being foreigners," he admitted. Then, "May I walk along with you?"

"It would be an honor."

There were questions, Chalem discovered, that he could ask Naomi that he hadn't been able to ask Ruth. His sense of freedom probably stemmed from the fact that Naomi was an Israelite, he realized, and so would have seen Moab with an Israelite's eyes. But he discovered as the conversation went on that while Naomi reported with fairness about Moab, she lacked Ruth's skill in description. Naomi didn't see the details that Ruth did and so could not impart them.

"Do you think Ruth likes it here?" he asked at last, planning to save his questions about Moab until he could talk to Ruth. "Do you think she's happy?"

He thought that Naomi would pass off his query with a light answer, but instead, she hesitated for a long time and then chose her words with a great deal of care.

"I don't know whether or not she's happy," Naomi said at last. "She's content enough, I think. I wish she didn't have to go out in the fields to glean, but she doesn't seem to mind. Your father has been very good to her."

"My father thinks she's good and beautiful just the way I do."

Once more, Naomi hesitated before she spoke. Then she said, "I, too, think she's good and beautiful. But — did your father tell you he thought so?"

"He didn't exactly say that. I just said that she was, and he said he agreed."

Naomi looked down at him. "You and your father were talking about Ruth?"

"Yes, I was asking him if he thought there was anyone who would be a go'el for her, and he said —" Chalem stopped so abruptly it was as though a hand had been clapped over his mouth.

"And he said?" Naomi prompted.

Chalem refused to meet her eyes. "Nothing. He didn't say anything."

They walked on in silence, and then Chalem announced, as though he had been figuring it all out in his head, "She should have a father-in-law to find the go'el, shouldn't she? Shiri's father-in-law did it for her. But Ruth doesn't have one."

"No, she doesn't," Naomi agreed. "She has only me."

"Women can't do anything," Chalem said. "Or at least, not out in the open, like the men who gather at the city gate. And, besides, Joamech might get angry,"

Naomi spoke quietly and carefully. "Joamech? The potter?"

"My father says he's the nearest relative."

Once more they were silent, and once more it was Chalem who broke the silence. "I told my father I'd pray to Yahweh about it." He couldn't tell this woman that he had planned to pray for a miracle so that Ruth wouldn't have to be married to Joamech. "But I — I didn't know how to begin."

"Just begin," Naomi said in a quick, decisive voice. "Just ask Yahweh to show me a way."

"You?"

"Ruth doesn't have a father-in-law," Naomi said simply. "You said so yourself. So it's up to me. And, as you said, I can't go to the elders of the city and demand a meeting at the city gate. I can only do — do what a woman can do."

Chalem stopped and stared up at her. "You don't want her to have to marry Joamech, either, do you?"

"I thought I did," Naomi confessed, "until I — well until I changed my mind. I'll make a pact with you if you like."

"A pact?"

"Yes. If you'll pray and if you'll try to figure out a way to persuade Aborakim that Ruth isn't so terrible, I'll try to figure out a way that she won't have to marry Joamech."

"It's a good pact," Chalem said judiciously. "Aborakim won't be easy. But I'll try."

"You do that." Naomi's voice was as flat and business-like as though she were bargaining with an adult. "And don't forget the prayers. They may be more important than anything else."

"I won't," Chalem promised. "I've got to hurry back now. My father may discover that I'm not taking the rest I was supposed to."

"Then hurry," Naomi said. "We don't want to upset your father."

Chalem shook his head and then turned to race toward home. He was almost there when his running slowed itself down to a walk. Naomi hadn't actually said that she would like to have his father as Ruth's go'el. Then why did he feel so certain that that was what she meant?

Ruth woke up from her nap, feeling light and refreshed. The privilege of resting during the day was so rare that she felt almost disoriented. She stretched and rolled over to gaze up into the leafy branches above her.

The fig tree was wholly beautiful, she thought. No other leaves were so broad and rich and green. Oh, she had seen fig trees stripped of their leaves by a voracious horde of locusts, but nothing seemed to threaten this lovely shelter which Yahweh had provided for them against the heat of the sun.

The sense of Yahweh's presence was as real, she discovered, as it had been during the night. Maybe, like the almond blossoms that had seemed to bloom overnight two months after Mahlon died, her faith had been growing all the time. If that were true, it wasn't so much that her faith blossomed last night but that she had become aware of the blossoming. Just as she had suddenly been aware of the almond blossoms.

She sat up and discovered that Naomi was sitting just outside the door gazing at the ground.

"Well, Mother," Ruth said. "I'm awake. And now you must rest and let me do everything that has to be done. The sun is low in the sky, so it must be time for dinner."

Naomi looked up. "I hope you're not very hungry. We don't have anything extra tonight. Just bread and some lentils. I'll be glad when the figs are ripe."

"It won't be long," Ruth said. "And, besides, I'm not as hungry as I am when I work all day. Bread and lentils sound fine."

"Then we'll eat. Everything's ready. And I don't need to rest. The walk I took was more refreshing than any sleep."

They talked lightly and casually during the meal, speaking most often of Altah's child. Naomi, too, had gone to see him, and, like Ruth, she was able to rejoice at the family's good fortune.

"They earned a blessing by the way they treated us," Naomi declared. "They took us in as willingly as though we had been kin to them, and their kindness has never ceased."

"Yahweh doesn't always reward goodness with blessing," Ruth reminded her. "Look at your faithfulness and how bitterly you were treated."

"True enough. We aren't supposed to understand such things. It's enough for now that Altah and Jacob have been blessed. Maybe such blessing will one day come to us."

Ruth looked up. "Maybe," she agreed and was afraid to say any more.

"Ruth," Naomi began. "I have something to suggest. I hope you'll hear me out before you make any protest."

Ruth stared at her mother-in-law without speaking. Naomi's color was high, and her eyes gleamed with excitement.

"While you slept," Naomi said, "I took a walk. And while I walked — I didn't go to see Elena after all — I think Yahweh spoke to me."

"Spoke to you? In words?"

"Not exactly. Although I do believe that sometimes Yahweh speaks to us through the words of other people. Do you think so?"

"I don't know, Mother. I'm only starting to know your God."

"Well, anyhow, I think Yahweh wants me to try to find a go'el for you."

The words jumped out at Ruth. "A go'el?" she stammered.

"Of course. Didn't I do as much for Orpah?"

"But — but it was different with Orpah. Mahlon was right there, Chilion's nearest kinsman. And he was willing."

"Not altogether willing," Naomi corrected her. "I had to do a great deal of persuading before he finally agreed. I never told you before he died because I was afraid you'd use it to defend your own unwillingness. And after he died — well —"

"Thank you, Mother. Thank you for telling me now. It makes me feel — more worthy, I guess."

"Worthy enough to try to get Boaz for a go'el?" Naomi asked.

Silence thrummed around them as they sat staring at each other.

"Boaz?" Ruth's whisper was faint.

"Of course. He's the one you want, isn't he?"

"But you said — you said Joamech was the nearest kinsman."

"He is, so, if we are to work this out, we must do it carefully. We can't offend Joamech."

"Oh, no." Ruth's voice was breathless. "My lord Boaz told me that he was hoping Joamech would serve as a master to teach Chalem pottery. Nothing must disturb their friendship."

"It presents problems," Naomi admitted. "But not insurmountable ones. I think — I believe — that if you do everything I tell you to, we can work it out."

"How?"

"I want you to bathe yourself (I brought extra jars of water so there would be enough) and put on perfume and your best clothes. You've never once worn that white shawl Mahlon bought for you from the trading caravan. You could wear that and we'll fix your hair as beautifully as possible."

"I'm dark from the sun, and my hair is brittle and dry." But Ruth's protest was automatic. She hardly realized what she had said.

"You're dark, it's true, but he'll understand that. And, as for your hair, I have some sweet oil warming near the fire. You can smooth it on your hair and braid a few fragrant flowers in it — there are a few ezob plants in blossom over there — and then — well, then you'll really be quite beautiful."

"And why am I to do this?"

"So that tonight you can go to the threshing floor and go to Boaz and tell him that you want him to be your go'el."

"Mother!" The exclamation was a sound of mingled shock and horror.

Naomi nodded with resolution. "Yes. Now listen to me. You can go down after dark and keep yourself hidden until the men have finished drinking and eating. They'll be tired and the wine will make them sleep soundly — so soundly a wolf howling won't wake them. Watch Boaz carefully to see where he lies down. And when he's asleep, you go over to him and lie down near his feet, covering yourself with his robe."

"Mother! You thought the orgies in Moab were sinful. And you *know* what kind of women go to the threshing floor. Now you're telling me to make myself one of them —"

"Indeed I'm not." Naomi's interruption was sharp. "Do you, yourself, think Boaz is the kind of man who would take advantage of a woman who came to him in such a way?"

Ruth had a clear image of Boaz' face, of the kind eyes that had met hers so often, of the gentle mouth. She thought of the way he greeted his workers, of the way he treated his sons. Oh, no, if ever there was a good man, it was Boaz.

"No," she said at last. "No, he would not take advantage of me."

"Then go," Naomi commanded. "I honestly believe that Yahweh has given me this plan."

Ruth stared at her mother-in-law for a long minute. "What about Joamech?" she finally whispered.

"Can't you leave something up to Yahweh? Can't you give Boaz any credit for being able to work things out?"

"Boaz? You mean he —?"

"I am absolutely sure," Naomi said firmly, "that Boaz cares for you. If you have enough faith and courage to do as I say, then who knows what wonders Yahweh will perform?"

For a long minute Ruth stared at her mother-in-law in silence. It is for this hour, she thought in awe, that Yahweh has given me the gift of faith. "I'll do it," she said to Naomi. "Will you help me get ready?"

Naomi rose with a smile of satisfaction, putting out her hand to pull Ruth to her feet. Ruth looked into the lined face. I was wrong to worry about whether I came with Naomi out of obedience or love, Ruth thought. I should have known all along that she and I are both acting out of love.

21

"THERE!" NAOMI STEPPED BACK and tilted her head. "You look lovely."

Ruth reached up to pull the filmy scarf more securely across her head and around her shoulders. "You're sure he won't think me brazen?"

Naomi's eyes twinkled. "I can think of many words I might use to describe you — stubborn, or strong, or even shy — but never brazen. I don't think, if you tried, you could be brazen."

"Well, but you know me better than he does."

"He knows something about you. He's been watching you in the fields. He can surely tell if you're the kind who would be indiscreet."

A slow wash of color spread up over Ruth's cheeks. "I don't know how," she confided. "Some of the women..." She stopped. "Well, some of them are not very discreet."

Naomi's voice was very brisk. "I'm sure. Now you'd better hurry. I don't want you on the road after dark."

"If it's not after dark," Ruth protested, "How can I remain hidden?"

"It's a problem," Naomi conceded. For long minutes she sat quietly, her brow furrowed. "I know," she said. "I'll walk with you to Elena's house. If anyone asks us, we'll say we need to talk to Elena about something. They live close to the threshing area, so while I'm talking you can slip out to their shed and hide there until the time is right."

"But if your sister and her daughter-in-law see me all dressed up and then if they see me slip out alone, you know what they'll think. They'll think I'm no better than — a harlot."

"Yes, I suppose you're right." Naomi's voice was heavy. "I thought I had everything all figured out, but you're right. Let me think."

"Mother." Ruth's voice was cautious. "Mother, do you honestly think this is Yahweh's plan for me? Do you truly believe He has spoken to you?"

Naomi's answer was strong and sure. "I'm positive. I prayed, and Yahweh sent — well, He sent words so clear that — "

"Words?" Ruth asked.

"Yahweh's words come in many ways," Naomi said firmly. "In the winds or in thoughts, or in the words of a child."

"Well then," Ruth said slowly, "if you truly believe that, I don't think we need to work out a scheme. I think we only have to put ourselves in His hands and trust Him."

"And you can do that?" There was both incredulity and hope in Naomi's voice.

"Yesterday I wouldn't have been able to do it, but today I can. I'll wait until it's almost dark, and then I'll throw that old black shawl around me so my light robe won't show up, and I'll just walk down to the threshing area and wait on the edge until Boaz is asleep."

"And you're not afraid?"

"Whether I'm afraid or not doesn't matter."

"Then," Naomi said, "I'll stay here and pray — and you, well, may you go in peace and safety."

Before darkness had fallen, Ruth was crouched in the scanty row of bushes that edged the threshing floor. Small fires burned here and there so that the large, flat area was fairly well lit in spite of the lateness of the hour.

The threshing floor itself was a large, high plateau where the earth had been scraped away so that, for the most part, naked stone formed a sort of floor. As Ruth watched, she saw Boaz and his men dumping dry grain into piles on the hard surface. Then, with much shouting, a team of unmuzzled oxen were driven onto the grain pulling a wide, heavy board with rough, sharp stones attached to the bottom for cutting and crushing the stalks.

Aborakim rode the heaving board, and she could not help but admire his agility and grace as he maintained his balance while providing the weight to hold the board down.

For what seemed a very long time, Ruth crouched stiff and aching in the darkest corner of the field, watching the activity. It was soon obvious to her that Boaz had generously allowed the other farmers to have their turn on the threshing floor first, and that he had waited until it was too dark to see what he was doing. What's more, the evening breeze, so brisk in the hours of dusk and first dark, were beginning to lessen.

Boaz' voice rang out finally. "Come, my son, enough. I'm sure the grain is sufficiently threshed. But it's too late for the winnowing. I'll wait until tomorrow evening so we'll have a brisker breeze to separate the chaff from the grain."

"We could have done it tonight if you hadn't let everyone get ahead of you," Aborakim said.

When Boaz spoke, he spoke with authority. "It was my decision to wait," Boaz answered. "You take the oxen to our shed and tie them for the night. Then stay at the house with your brother." He raised his voice. "Chalem!"

The boy came running from a group by one of the fires.

"Chalem," Boaz said, "go with Aborakim. First, help him unharness the oxen. Then go with him to stable the beasts and after that, both of you go to bed."

"Can't we come back here to sleep?" Chalem's voice was pleading.

"Not tonight. Perhaps when we winnow the wheat. Tonight, I'll sleep here to protect the crop. Only one person is needed. Here — just help me push our grain out of the way so other men can use the threshing floor tomorrow. We'll be first in line for the winnowing when the evening breeze comes up."

The boys helped him shove the dusty, broken stalks to one side, and then Aborakim led the oxen toward the opposite side of the field, his father and brother following him. Although Chalem's pleading to stay all night went on, Ruth could no longer hear the words. She shifted cautiously, pulling back even farther into the shadows. The fact that she was still undetected seemed right and natural to her. Still there was no point in being too close to the light of the fires.

She watched Chalem and Aborakim leave and was grateful to see that although Aborakim was plainly irritated with his assigned tasks, he did not bully his younger brother. There is much of Boaz in his older son, Ruth thought. I wish there were some way that I could change his hatred for me into tolerance. If, just once, he could look at me simply as a woman, not as a Moabite, I would dare to hope.

She was very cramped and cold before the fires finally died down to coals. Then men had talked and sung for a long time, their boisterous and bawdy jokes loud in the night. Ruth began to wonder if the wineskins would ever stop making the rounds. But, gradually, the noise ceased as the men found places to lie down. Ruth watched as, like the others, Boaz stretched out on his robe. She was grateful that he chose to lie down in an isolated spot. Like the others, he was asleep almost immediately.

When silence finally lay heavy over the threshing floor, Ruth got to her feet. For one terrifying moment, she let her mind touch on the things that could happen to her during the next few minutes. If she had misjudged Boaz, or if one of the other farmers was awake and saw her, then this night could end in disgrace or rape or even death for her.

"Yahweh, my God," she breathed and was given the courage to walk over to where Boaz lay sleeping.

What had Naomi said? To lie down by his feet. To simply lie down and leave the rest up to Yahweh and to Boaz. Well, then, she would do exactly as she had been bidden. And if the night ended in tragedy for her, why, then, so be it.

Cautiously, quietly, she lowered herself to the ground, spreading out her dark shawl so she could lie on an edge of it and pull the rest of it around her. With gentle hands, she lifted the edge of Boaz' robe, and as Naomi had instructed, pulled it over her. For a minute she held her breath, but Boaz never stirred. She heard only the deep breathing that told of his fatigue.

She felt a fleeting wish to cradle his head against her shoulder so that he might have a sort of pillow. And then, in spite of her belief that she could not possibly sleep under these circumstances, a great wave of stillness and peace flowed over her and she drifted into sleep.

The night was half gone when Boaz, apparently waking stiff and cramped, sat up to stretch his body. His movement disturbed Ruth, and she turned over, sighing deeply. Startled, Boaz leaned forward and spoke quickly, "Who is this?"

Ruth, fully awake at the sound of his voice, hurried to say words of reassurance. "It's only I, Ruth, your maid."

"What are you doing here?" Shock and dismay roughened his voice.

"Please, my lord, please listen to me." She kept her voice very soft so that they would disturb no one else. "I came because my mother-in-law told me to come. I would never have dared come otherwise, my lord. She told me that you are a close kinsman and that perhaps —" Her voice faltered and she took a deep breath, "Perhaps you would — well, spread your covering over me."

There was a long silence, but she could hear the quiet, unhurried sound of his breathing, a sharp contrast to the rapid, uneven breath that caught in her throat.

"You want me to be your go'el?" he asked at last.

He will surely judge me brazen and shameless, she thought, but it was too late now to retreat.

"Yes, my lord," she whispered, wishing desperately she could see him. He was only a darker shape against the dark sky. What expression was on his face, she could not even guess.

"I'm a great deal older than you," he said, but his voice was mild.

She had expected anger or disgust or shock. This small bit of logic shattered her hard-held composure.

"Oh, my lord," she choked, feeling the tears spilling over her cheeks. "Oh, my lord, if you were fifty years older than I, I would still be unworthy of you."

Boaz' hands groped toward her in the dark, and, sensing the movement, she put out her own hands to him. She knew that her hands were not small and soft as a lady's hands should be. Her hands, like the rest of her, were large and capable, the fingers and palms now roughened by the gleaning. But Boaz' hands were larger, rougher, and they held hers with gentleness and strength.

His voice, when he spoke, was still a whisper, but she heard a new note in it, a quickened sound. "May the Lord bless you," he said, "for not looking at younger men. You're beautiful enough that you could have almost anyone, it seems to me."

"I, my lord? I never even thought about it. From the first hour that I saw your face, I have seen no one else."

"Nor I. From the minute you looked up at me, I have thought of nothing but you."

"Oh, my lord, I never guessed —"

"That I wanted you? Naomi must have guessed. Aborakim did."

"Your son hates me, my lord."

"He thinks he does. My son is young and arrogant and proud. He has told everyone who would listen that he hates all Moabites. It would be hard on his pride to admit he might be wrong."

In order to keep the sound of their voices undetected, they continued to speak in the softest of whispers, and almost automatically drew closer together. Ruth felt Boaz' breath on her cheek, and her heart seemed to tumble erratically. She had never, she reflected dazedly, felt just this way with Mahlon.

He must have been equally aware of her nearness because he moved suddenly and she heard his breath quicken. "Why are we talking about Aborakim?" he said and pulled her into his arms. He bent his head and his lips found hers.

Oh, surely, surely, her heart sang, this must mean that he is willing to marry me, that it is only a matter of words now, of action taken. Sighing, she let her mouth soften and respond to his kiss.

He held her closer, letting his lips move over her face and throat. Then, abruptly, he pulled himself away.

"I have no right," he said, breathing hard. "No matter how I have longed to do just that, I have no right."

"No right, my lord?"

"No. I'm not your nearest kinsman."

"I know." Her voice was dull. "Joamech is."

"You know about him? Oh, yes, I remember. We spoke of him the day we met on the way to the fields."

"And you want him to train Chalem to be a potter. I know."

Boaz put his arms around her again and drew her close, but there was restraint in the gesture. "You think," he whispered in her ear, "you think I would yield to him because I need to keep his friendship? You think I'd give up my claim on you just for that? You wrong me, my dear."

"Why else then? If you — if you're willing to serve as my go'el and if I — if I love you as I do, then why must Joamech even be considered?"

"Because it's the law."

"The law. I'm not even an Israelite. Why must the law control *me*?"

"The law is of Yahweh and from Yahweh. It is His way of protecting the family."

Her rebellion dissolved as quickly as it had flared up. "I'm sorry, my lord. I came to you in the conviction that Yahweh wanted me to come. If He doesn't really want me to belong to you, I'll accept it. But, please, my lord, must I marry a man who already has a wife in his house?"

Boaz laughed silently. "I'll make every effort to see that you marry no one but me."

"But what about Joamech?"

"Can't you trust me to work it out?"

"If I didn't trust you, my lord, would I have come to you in this place, in the middle of the night?"

"And I'm grateful." Boaz' voice was humble.

"Then, my lord, I'll leave it up to you — to you and to your God. I'll rest in your hands and His."

"You didn't always think of Him as a refuge," Boaz reminded her.

"I know. I've learned a great deal since I came to Bethlehem. Most of it, my lord, I learned from you. I came to believe that your kindness and generosity must be because the God you worshiped was merciful and good."

Boaz was silent, but his arms were warm and secure, more of a shelter against the night than any walls could be. For a few seconds Ruth let herself lean against him, then, knowing she dare not lean too much on his nearness and his strength, she gently pulled herself away.

"I'm sorry I disturbed your rest, my lord. It was just that Naomi said..." She made a move to get up. "I'll leave you now."

"No. It's too dark. You'll stumble and fall. Or worse things could happen. You know there are wild animals out there. But they won't come near the fires. Just lie down again. Here, take my robe and pull it over you against the chill."

"But, my lord —"

"No, do as I tell you. If you're going to be my wife, you'll have to get used to obeying me." There was a thread of laughter in his voice.

"I'll wake you just before dawn, he promised. "You don't have to worry anymore about anything."

'Yes, my lord." She lay down as he had told her to, and although he lay scrupulously away from her, he reached across the space between them to capture her hand in his.

"Sleep," he whispered. And then, faint as a breath came the words she had longed to hear. "Sleep well, my love, my dear one."

You, too, my lord," she whispered and silence fell between them.

She was almost asleep when she was stabbed with a sudden realization. She had told him of her love without fear, without hesitation, without reticence. Never before in her life had she dared to do and say the sort of things she had done and said this night.

Oh, thank you, Yahweh, she thought. And with no further fear for the morrow, she closed her eyes and slept.

22

THE FIRST LIGHT of dawn was barely perceptible when
Ruth felt Boaz' hand on her cheek. She was tempted to turn
her face and touch her lips to his palm, but something held
her back. There was, after all, no guarantee that she could
ever be his wife.

"I'm awake, my lord," she whispered.

"Be as quiet as possible," he warned. "I don't want anyone to know that you were here. Come, I'll walk with you to
the road."

They got up from the ground, not touching. In spite of
her confidence of the night before, Ruth felt strangely lonely and none of the memories of Boaz' words or of his touch
did anything to comfort her.

"Wait." Boaz' soft command stopped her. "I want you to
take grain to Naomi. May I have your shawl?"

Quietly, she unwound it from her shoulders and handed
it to him. Boaz worked in silence and then handed the
heavy, bulky bundle to Ruth. "Can you carry it? I've given
you enough so that you won't go to your mother-in-law
empty-handed."

"Thank you, my lord." Her voice was toneless. She
wanted to tell him that she might not go home empty-
handed, but she would surely go empty-hearted. She had
dreamed of taking home a promise, but she had only a
hope.

"Perhaps the amount will show Naomi how much I appreciate her thinking of me," he said.

They had reached the road and stood far enough away from the threshing area that they dared speak in a more normal voice.

"She'll be grateful, my lord."

"You sound so dispirited. Are you sorry that you came?"

"No, my lord, not sorry. That is, I'm not if you aren't."

Boaz laughed softly. "I? I feel as young as a boy. Tell me something. Is Naomi willing to sell the field that was Elimilech's?"

"Oh, yes, my lord. She had hoped to offer it to you but had decided that in order to obey the law, she'd have to offer it to Joamech. It's a very valuable field, my lord."

"Valuable enough." The words were casual, but Boaz' voice was excited. "Well, leave it to me, my dear. The field may one day yet come to your son, as it should."

She stood staring through the near darkness, straining to see his face clearly.

"To your son and mine," Boaz whispered, touching her face. "If Yahweh will hear my prayers, there may be such a boy some day."

"I've been barren, my lord," she choked out, "I can't promise I could bear a son."

"Ah, but with the Lord, nothing is impossible," Boaz promised. "Don't you know the story of Sarah who bore a child when she was old? And you're still young."

"If I can be your wife, my lord," she dared to say, "then I will pray every day of my life that Yahweh will give us a son."

"But, first," Boaz said, "you must pray that I can persuade the elders of the town that I should be your go'el. I, not Joamech."

She felt the cold touch of fear again. "Yes, my lord."

"Then hurry home," he said. "And remember that if I can redeem you, I will."

He gave her a gentle push toward town. Because her

arms were full, she could not put out her hand to the man facing her. She could only nod dumbly and then turn toward home.

"Can you see the road?" he asked.

"Yes, my lord. I can see it well enough."

"Then go in peace."

She did not even try to look back. She hurried along the dirt road weighed down, at first, by equally heavy burdens of grain and grief. Then, slowly, to her surprise, the heavy feeling of despondency which had filled her on waking began to lighten. What was it Boaz had said? That with the Lord nothing was impossible. Well, then, she would hold onto that.

"Oh, praise be! You're home!"

Ruth looked up, startled. She had been plodding along, so involved in her thoughts, so weighed down by the load in her arms, that she was unaware of how far she had come. Naomi was standing outside the shed, the anxiety on her face discernible in the light of dawn.

"Haven't you slept?" Ruth asked, staggering a little from fatigue.

Naomi shrugged. "Who could sleep? Here, let me help you. You've used your good shawl."

"He asked for it. Boaz asked for it."

Naomi looked up sharply, the lines of anxiety suddenly deepened. "He gave you so much? He's never been so generous before."

Ruth spoke quickly. "Don't worry. It's not what you might think. He asked nothing of me."

Naomi nodded with satisfaction. "See, I knew he would be kind. And good. What did he say to you?"

Although they had been speaking in very soft tones, Ruth cast a worried look over her shoulder. "When we're inside," she whispered, "then I'll tell you everything."

"Well, come then, Naomi commanded. "It's been a very long night."

They walked into the shed, and Ruth dropped wearily to

the floor. While Naomi poured the grain into storage jars, Ruth told her everything that had happened.

"So you see," Ruth concluded. "I don't know anything now that I didn't know before."

"You know that he cares for you."

"Yes," Ruth said slowly. "I know that."

"Well, then, if he can work it out, he will. And before this day is over, I'm sure."

"I know what Patima would say," Ruth said, getting up. "She'd tell me to go out to the fields to work and leave my worries at home."

"Good advice!" Naomi's voice was firm. "You work and I'll worry."

They smiled at each other, and then Naomi opened her arms, and Ruth fled into them. Neither of them said anything. They held each other for a few minutes before Ruth pulled herself away to begin her preparations for going out to glean.

Chalem woke with the guilty feeling that he had slept too late. To his relief, he saw that Aborakim was still curled into a tight ball, his head buried under a coverlet.

At least, Chalem thought, if I'm late, we're both late. He stretched out his leg and dug his toe into his brother's back. Aborakim snorted and jerked away.

"The sun is up," Chalem announced. "Father will be furious with both of us."

Aborakim stretched and yawned. "Then why are you still lying there? Why aren't you up and on your way to the fields?"

"I'm waiting to help you harness up the oxen."

Aborakim sat up and rubbed his hands through his hair. "You aren't always so considerate," he observed. "Why are you trying to earn my approval?"

"What's your approval to me?" Chalem asked, but he was remembering his promise to Naomi. He might be more likely to persuade Aborakim that Ruth was a worthy person if he were a little less cocky. He ducked his head and eyed his older brother. "Well, I don't want to start out the day by making you mad at me."

"Then go and tell one of the kitchen girls — Dori is more generous than the other — to have some bread and cheese ready for us in a few minutes. And don't leave your cover strewn all over the floor so I trip on it as I usually do."

Meekly, Chalem bent and retrieved his rumpled cover. He folded it neatly and laid it on his sleeping mat before he headed for the kitchen.

He had spent half the night — well, perhaps not half the night, but a long time — trying to come up with a plan that would alter Aborakim's attitude toward Ruth. So far, he had thought of nothing. And his prayer had been such a childish, disjointed thing. What would the God of Jacob and Isaac make of a silly prayer like, "Please, Lord, don't let Joamech want her."

He delivered Aborakim's message and then waited listlessly until his brother appeared. They ate in haste, and after harnessing the oxen, made their way to the threshing floor.

Boaz was waiting for them. "The blessing of Yahweh be with you," he greeted them warmly enough, but his next words were sharp. "You're late."

"I didn't wake up," Chalem confessed before Aborakim could say anything. He saw the look of astonishment on his big brother's face. "I planned to wake at dawn but I failed."

"Well, never mind," Boaz said. "Listen, I have some errands for you to do. Aborakim, you stay here to guard the grain and to offer the oxen to any poor farmer who has no animals."

Aborakim looked at his father and smiled. "If you're not careful," he said mockingly, "you'll be making me as benevolent as you. Then who will guard our assets?"

Boaz grinned. "No danger," he said and turned to his younger son. "Run over to the house of Joamech, the potter. See if he can come by the city gate sometime this morning. I'll wait there for him."

Chalem's eyes began to sparkle. "Joamech?" he asked eagerly. "What do you want to talk to him about? Are you going to ask him to teach me to be a potter?"

"What business is it of yours what your father plans to do?" Aborakim's voice was sharp. "You started out the day so well. Can't you keep it up for even an hour?"

Chalem opened his mouth and then slowly closed it. "I'm sorry," he murmured with a great show of contrition and was rewarded with another look of astonishment on Aborakim's face. Maybe it was really true, as his father had always claimed, that soft words acomplished more than blows.

"Now, hurry," Boaz said. "And then go and tell the overseer I won't be out in the fields today. I have business at the city gates."

"Yes, Father," Chalem said. His heart had begun beating wildly, because he was remembering that day when a meeting at the city gates had brought a go'el for Shiri. Is that why his father was requesting the presence of the potter? Perhaps, Joachem was to be asked to be Ruth's go'el, after all. If that happened, his dream of having his father marry Ruth would never come true. In his dismay and fear, all his good resolutions went flying. He crossed his eyes, stuck out his tongue and made a rude gesture to Aborakim, but before that young man could react, Chalem was flying across the city toward the home of Joamech.

Behind him, his father and older brother looked at each other.

"Surely I was never so insolent when I was young," Aborakim said in a voice that barely escaped being pompous.

"You had no older brother to be insolent to," Boaz said. "But, if my memories don't fail me, the servants suffered a great deal more at your hands than they do at Chalem's."

Aborakim grinned with a shamed look. "Perhaps he'll learn better manners when he grows up."

"Learning any new thing," Boaz said slowly, "or letting your mind grow, or even having the courage to change your mind — these are all part of growing up." He looked as though he wanted to say more, but he was silent.

Finally, he started to leave, then changed his mind and turned again to Aborakim. "You are my first born," he said, "and so the one I must trust. You should know that I'm going to the city gate to persuade the elders of the city to let me marry Ruth."

"The Moabite?" Aborakim's voice was thin.

"Ruth, the Moabite. I have learned to love her. I want her for my wife."

The boy's knuckles were white on the oxen reins. "But Joamech is the nearest kinsman."

"Joamech already has a wife."

"So had you, my father."

"Your mother was a good woman, and I was a good husband to her. She gave me two fine sons who delight my heart. But I'm alone and still young enough to father sons."

"Sons who might take your love away from us. Sons who would be brought up to be Moabite savages."

Boaz stared at his son. "I won't waste my words," he said at last. "If you've watched Ruth in our fields for all these days, and you're still blind to her gentleness and goodness, then no words of mine will change your mind. If, indeed," he added wearily, "you are grown up enough to ever have the courage to change your mind about an idea that just might possibly have been wrong from the beginning."

He turned on his heel and left Aborakim staring after him. For a long time the boy stood still, his hands taut on the leather reins. Then, as though he had suddenly made up his mind, he sought out a trusted friend and asked him to guard their grain. Turning the heads of the oxen toward home, he followed them across the fields, unharnessed them and led them into a field to graze. Hurrying into the house, he put on a robe more suitable than the one he had worn to work in the fields. Then, although he knew he was disobeying his father's orders for the day, he headed for the council benches at the city gate.

23

CHALEM HAD NEARLY REACHED Joamech's house when he saw Ruth hurrying along the street that led to the edge of town and his father's fields. For a minute he was tempted to call to her and perhaps even tell her of his errand. But that would be foolish, he quickly reasoned. Whatever happened today at the city gate was not Ruth's concern. Like all women, she simply had a task to do while the men of the town decided her fate.

Chalem felt a sense of satisfaction with the fact that that was the way life was. The next thought came into his mind with the suddenness of early winter rain. He was only ten, but he was also a male of the village. He, too, had a responsibility. He was to pray, Naomi had said, and try to win Aborakim over. Chalem remembered the ugly face he had made at his brother and felt immediate regret. Was his concern for Ruth so slight that he could forget his duty at the first sense of irritation or uncertainty?

His steps slowed as his mind worked faster and faster, probing the depth of his feeling about Ruth. Hadn't his childish prayers been simply a request for Ruth as though she were an object he wanted — like a new slingshot or a donkey of his own? Had he even thought of what might be best for Ruth?

He came to a halt and stared down at his dusty feet. Surely it would be best for Ruth to be married to his father,

199

to be a mother to him and Aborakim, wouldn't it? Or would it?

Reluctantly, he remembered the gray in his father's hair, he thought of his own indolence and occasional insolence, he heard Aborakim's voice saying furiously, "She's a Moabite and I hate her!"

But in our house, she would have food and pretty clothes and even silver bracelets, he argued with that part of his mind which had dredged up such painful thoughts.

She would have that in Joamech's house, too, responded the honest part of him. Oh, maybe the potter was not nearly as rich as Boaz, but he was comfortable. And his children were young. They wouldn't react to Ruth as Aborakim had.

"O Lord," Chalem whispered in a desolate voice, "I'm sorry I've been so selfish. Just give Ruth what is best for her."

He stood a few seconds fighting an unmanly stinging in his eyes, then shook his head and started to walk swiftly toward the potter's shop.

The room was dim, and Chalem stood for a little while inside the door.

"What are you doing out so early in the morning, son of Boaz?" The voice was hearty and condescending. "Have you broken another water jar and has your father sent you to replace it?"

Chalem shook his head. "I'm not as clumsy as I used to be," he said. "I bring my father's greetings to my lord Joamech."

The potter, thin and stooped, grinned at the little boy. "Is he still harvesting the crops?"

"The barley is all harvested and we're beginning the threshing. They're still harvesting the wheat."

"They? You're not helping?

"Oh, yes, of course. But I don't like it much."

"No?" Joamech beckoned to draw the child closer. "Then what *do* you like? Running and playing?"

"I would like to be a potter."

I shouldn't have said it, Chalem thought with a sense of dismay. I should have let my father make the first move. I should have just nodded my head. Why am I so foolish?

Joamech looked both astonished and pleased. "A potter? You think it would be easier?"

"Oh, no, my lord. Probably harder. But I love the feel of clay in my hands. I've even tried to make pots. I'm not very good, but I'd like to learn." Since he had admitted his desire to be a potter, there was nothing to be gained by silence now.

Joamech nodded. "It's possible that you have the feeling. Many of our kinsmen have had it. Elimelech, his sons, my father and I, myself. Is this what you came to tell me?"

"Oh, no, my lord, I've come to ask you to meet my father at the city gate. Could you do that this morning? He would be grateful."

Joamech stood considering. "Let me think. I have no pots in the oven just now, so I don't have to worry about the fire in the kiln. And I haven't started wedging a new batch of clay. This might be a good morning for me. Tell your father I'll be there by midmorning."

"Oh, thank you, my lord. I'll go and tell him."

The boy looked around the room, his eyes now accustomed to the dimness. With a longing that was almost an ache in him, he stared at the bin of clay, at the wheel with its traces of earth, at the finished pots that filled the shelves.

"We'll talk about your desire to be a potter," Joamech promised. Perhaps that's what your father wishes to see me about."

"I don't know, my lord," Chalem stammered, wondering if he was lying. After all, his father had not told him the purpose of the meeting. It was only his own worry which had suggested that there would be talk of a go'el for Ruth. "I'll hurry and take your message. My father will be waiting for you, my lord."

"Good." Joamech sounded cheerful and indifferent. He

had turned back to his work almost before Chalem had run out the door.

He would be an easy man to work for, Chalem thought, and if he's the man Yahweh wants to be Ruth's husband, then at least I can see her sometimes. But the thought was no solace at all.

By midmorning, Boaz had contrived to gather together ten of the men of Bethlehem. The men, for the most part, were the scholars, teachers, and elders of the town, men who spent their days reading and talking. Most of them were old, but they were highly respected and there were none in Bethlehem who would question their decisions.

Boaz sat among them quietly, so quietly that none of them realized that he was the one who had gathered them together. If he spoke at all, it was just to applaud another's comment.

Only one man questioned Boaz' presence at the gate, and that was old Eli. He was too old now to herd sheep, too old to do anything but sit and nod in the sun, and ponder the Law.

"You're not in the fields, my son? Is the harvest finished then?"

"Not yet, my father. I have left my work in the hands of my sons."

Eli's head moved in a palsied nod. "Blessed is the man who has sons to follow in his steps."

Boaz, who had caught a glimpse of Aborakim behind the wall, who knew that Chalem was playing with a group of urchins down the street, smiled. "Yes," he agreed. "A man cannot have too many sons. Do you agree?"

For a few seconds Eli's voice was almost as firm as it had been in his youth. "It's a man's duty to have sons. The Law states it plainly."

"How wise you are," Boaz murmured and looked up to see his cousin, Joamech, hurrying along the street that led to the gate. If Boaz felt any apprehension, there was no sign of it. His hands lay still in his lap, and his eyes were serene.

"Greetings, cousin," Boaz called out in a steady voice. "The peace of Yahweh be with you."

"And with you." Joamech's smile was wide. "Your younger son said you would like to see me, so I came."

"I'm glad. There are several things I want to discuss with you. But, first, come and sit. Tell me how the pottery business goes."

"Well enough." Joamech dropped onto the bench lining the square room that formed a gate to the city wall. "There's always a need for water pots and storage jars. Particularly at harvest time."

"One of my kitchen girls brought home a new jar the other day from your pottery. I've put it in a corner of the main room because it's too pretty for the kitchen."

"I'm glad if it pleased you, my cousin." Joamech's smile broadened further.

Boaz spoke casually, as though the words were unimportant. "My younger son — Chalem — thinks he would like to be a potter. It's only natural, I suppose. There have been many potters in our family."

"But they're never as rich as the farmers in the family," Joamech said modestly.

"What is richness?" Boaz asked conversationally. "You create articles of both beauty and practical value. You feed the eye and the hands. I feed the belly with my grain. I may have more land, but you must have great satisfaction in your heart."

"As you say." Joamech sounded pleased.

"Your son," Boaz began, "he's too young to know, I suppose, but will he follow in your steps?"

"He'd rather play in the mud than anything else. If that's any indication, he'll probably be a potter."

"And the rest of your children are daughters —?"

"All of them. And all of them as willful as their mother."

The two men exchanged a look of amusement. In a village as small as Bethlehem, one could not help but know something of the temper of Joamech's wife. A good woman, Boaz was remembering, but one a husband would hesitate to cross.

"Then — if there are no other sons, do you suppose you would consider taking an apprentice?"

"Chalem?"

"Yes, Chalem."

Boaz had seen, out of the corner of his eye, the stealthy approach of Chalem. He had expected the child's face to be blazing with excitement at the way the conversation was going, but Chalem seemed to be thinking about something else.

Joamech spread out his hands. "It might work. Even if there should be another son for me, it would be years before he'd be able to tramp or wedge the clay. Is the boy strong?"

"Stronger than he knows," Boaz answered. "He might find it hard at first, but he'd soon adjust."

"My kinsman, Elimelech, was a potter," Eli piped up in a querulous voice. "He went to Moab, though. Many and many a year ago."

Joamech grinned, but Boaz' voice was gentle. "Yes, my father. Elimelech was skillful beyond words."

"It isn't always easy to make ends meet," Joamech interposed. "My wife and I are hard put to have good food on the table. You wouldn't expect the boy to stay at night, would you?"

"Not when he lives such a short distance away," Boaz said. "And I'd plan to share the produce of my fields with you. To pay for his training, there would be meal and oil, olives and cheese. I'd make it worth your while."

Joamech beamed. "I'd be lying, my cousin, if I didn't admit such generosity would help. We don't all own land, you know."

"I know. And that reminds me —" Boaz kept his voice casual, but he was as aware of his own quickened heart beat as he was of the sudden tension and stillness in both of his listening sons. "You know, don't you, that Naomi, the widow of Elimelech, has a field to sell?"

Joamech's eyes narrowed as he licked his lips. "No, I didn't know. You mean the high field beyond the stone boundary? That one?"

"Yes. As you probably know, Elimelech's brother kept it in trust for many years, but he's dead now. And both of Naomi's sons are dead. Since there are no grandchildren, the field will be sold to the nearest kinsman. So, if you want it, if you feel you can buy it, the field is yours."

Joamech forgot about the inability to put food on his table. "I think I could manage it," he said eagerly. "My father-in-law would help me raise the price. Yes, I'd like to have it."

"Well, that's fine," Boaz said. "I'll tell her — Naomi, that is — and make arrangements for you two to settle the deal."

"Most potters don't have fields," Eli protested thinly.

"Most potters don't have two wives either," Boaz said easily, "but there are always exceptions. Right, my cousin?"

Joamech looked stunned. "Two wives? What do you mean? Am I expected to marry Elimelech's widow? But she's old enough to be my mother."

Boaz smiled. "Oh, no, not Naomi. Her daughter-in-law. Ruth the Moabite."

Eli's cackle split the sudden silence. "Ai, and isn't she the pretty one? Tall as a queen and dark as an Egyptian. I've seen her in the fields, I have."

"Hush, old man." One of the men remonstrated in embarrassment. "Don't talk so lightly of a woman who gave up everything for her mother-in-law — a woman whose cleverness saved your nephew, Jacob, and Jacob's unborn son from certain death when they were attacked by thieves on their journey from Moab."

A murmur of approval ran through the assembled men, and Boaz felt an unexpected stab of fear. If Joamech were led to believe that Ruth was a prize....

But Joamech was obviously thinking of something else. "I already have one wife," he mumbled. "I'm not sure I want another."

"That Ruth, she won't spit fire at you," Eli shrilled. "She'd be more like shade on a hot day."

Joamech gazed from face to face, his mouth hanging open, his eyes bewildered. "But she's a Moabite," he managed to say.

Boaz said nothing. He merely waited.

"And the field," Joamech asked at last. "The field of Elimelech. It would go to her son who would bear Mahlon's name, wouldn't it? It wouldn't go to my own boy."

"It would go to Ruth's son, if she should bear a son," Boaz answered. "And the child would be the son of Mahlon, under the Law."

"My wife wouldn't like it," Joamech muttered and glared defiantly at Eli's derisive laughter. "Nor would I. My boy's the joy of my life. I wouldn't want him cheated out of my only field."

"You aren't forced to take her," Boaz said softly. "I'm the next in line, and I have no wife to object. What's more, I already have many fields to go to my older son, so what is one more field to me — or to him?"

He didn't look toward the place where he knew Aborakim was standing, but he was very much aware of the boy's stillness.

"All right, then, you take her," Joamech said.

"I don't want to cheat you, my cousin," Boaz said in protest. "I'm looking forward to your working with my son. I wouldn't want to have you think later I've cheated you."

"Cheated me?" Joamech let out a guffaw of laughter. "Saved me a thousand hours of yammering, I'd guess. There may be men who can handle two women. But not me."

"You'll make the sign of contract?" Boaz asked.

Joamech bent and fumbled with his sandal. Taking it from his foot, he thrust it toward Boaz. "Take her with my blessing," he said. "And when the harvest is finished, send the boy to me. I'll work him till he'll wish he was back in the fields, but he has the feel for it. I could tell. If he can stand the wedging and my wife's tongue, I'll make a potter of him."

Boaz looked around at the men who lined the benches. "You've heard my cousin?" he asked. "You accept this as a binding word that the field of Elimelech is mine — and also Mahlon's widow?"

The man who had scolded Eli nodded. "We've heard. I speak for all my brethren when I say the contract is sound."

Boaz smiled with relief. "Then it shall be done. With your agreement that I have observed the law, I'll take Ruth, the widow of Mahlon, as my wife."

"Had we wine," old Eli said wistfully, "we could drink to it."

Chalem tumbled into the center of the men, his cheeks scarlet, his eyes shining. "I'll get some, Father. May I? It's only a few steps to our house."

"Then go, my son. Tell Dori to give you the wineskin that's cool. And bring a cup. We'll drink to my cousin's wisdom and discretion."

"And to life," Joamech said.

"May she be like Rachel and Leah," Eli said, grinning. "May she give you many sons and may they bring richness to you. Has the boy come yet with the wine?" he finished hopefully.

There was a sound of laughter, but although Boaz joined in the sound of joy, his eyes were anxiously scanning the crowd. Aborakim had been there behind that corner of the wall only a minute ago. Now he was gone.

Chalem came racing back, the wineskin swinging precariously from his hand. "Here, Father, here it is."

The cup was passed from hand to hand, and the congratulatory cries were warm. At first, Chalem laughed with the men, but gradually he became aware of his father's anxiety.

"Are you looking for Aborakim?" he asked shrewdly.

Boaz nodded.

"I'll go find him," the little boy said. He leaned close to his father and whispered, "Don't worry. If Yahweh gave Ruth to us, He can straighten out Aborakim. Just wait and see."

24

RUTH HAD EXPECTED the day of waiting for Boaz's decision to be one of mental turmoil and agony. To her astonishment, the depression of the pre-dawn hours had not returned in spite of the fact that she felt no real confidence that Boaz would be able to persuade the elders to let him serve as her go'el. After all, she had done nothing to deserve such a happy ending to her problems. She had been jealous of Mahlon, she had been reticent with everyone who mattered to her, she had been slow to develop any real faith in the Lord God Yahweh.

But none of these things seemed to matter. Even if she had to remain a lonely widow for the rest of her life, she might grieve but she would not despair. The knowledge that Boaz *wanted* to marry her, the certainty that Yahweh cared for her were comfort enough. Somehow she would manage even if she were forced to marry Joamech.

She worked silently, rhythmically, picking up the small piles of wheat that had fallen from the sickles of the reapers, and while she worked, her mind slid back over the year just past. She thought of Patima, remembering the sturdy wholesomeness of her, the merriment and the strength. She left her mind touch on Orpah and Mahlon, and she knew that nothing would change the fact that once she had loved them.

As though she were naming her blessings, she thought of Naomi, of Shiri, Chalem, Altah and Jacob and their new baby. She looked up from her gleaning and met the smiles of others who were working in the field. How short a time ago she had been a stranger, a foreigner in a foreign land.

I've been given so much, Ruth thought humbly. I have no right to ask for more.

The sun was high in the sky, and Ruth had just straightened up to ease her aching back when she heard the familiar greeting flow across the field.

"The peace of the Lord be with you."

It was Boaz. For a few seconds she was afraid, but then she forced herself to look toward him. If he avoided her eyes, if —

But he was obviously looking for her, and when their eyes met, his smile was wide. She had thought she would be calm, no matter which way the decision had gone. But she found that her breath caught in her throat and that her knees were trembling.

"My lord," she murmured as Boaz came near.

"Greetings, my daughter." His voice was casual, unhurried. Only the brightness of his eyes betrayed his excitement, and he was careful to look only at her. "Will you carry a message for me?"

"Of course, my lord," she whispered.

"Will you tell your mother-in-law that I will be happy to buy her husband's field? Tell her I will assume all the responsibility that accompanies the purchase."

"You mean, my lord, that — " She could hardly say the words.

"And tell her that I will come tonight to talk to her. She and I will make arrangements for the wedding that will take place. The marriage of her daughter-in-law to Boaz of Bethlehem."

She stood staring at him, feeling the heat of her blood in her face.

"I'll tell her, my lord."

"And now, go home. It's not fitting that my wife should be a gleaner in the fields."

"Yes, my lord." There were a hundred questions clamoring to be asked, but this was not the time to ask them. There was only one she could not restrain. "Your son, my lord? Aborakim, I mean."

"He knows. He disobeyed me and came to the city gates, so he knows what happened. I don't know where he is."

"Perhaps he's angry, my lord."

"My son does not have the right to be angry with me. He'll be home before dark."

She shook her head slowly. "I wish he didn't hate me," she murmured.

"We'll talk of it later," he said. "Go now as I've told you."

"Yes, my lord." Automatically, she stooped for the bundle of grain. When Boaz would have taken it from her, she shook her head. "No, my lord, let me take home the amount I've gathered. My mother-in-law will like the feeling of plenty. Even though she won't need it anymore if she's to move into your house."

Gratefully, she saw that her words seemed to be only what Boaz expected. "Then tell her to enjoy her last days in the shed before she moves into a household of boys and men."

Ruth smiled. "She's used to it, my lord. She reared two sons. She'll be the happiest woman in Bethlehem."

"The second happiest, I hope," Boaz said very quietly, and Ruth felt her cheeks grow warm again.

"Yes, my lord," she said in a tone of agreement. She turned, then, and started walking away from the field where she had found food for her need and joy for her heart.

When she came to the fork in the path, she hesitated a minute. Ever since the day Boaz had warned her of the dangers of the shorter path, she had obediently taken the long way home. But today, in her state of excitement, she wanted only to get home as quickly as possible so that she might tell Naomi her news. Surely if she were careful, she would be all right. Holding the bundle of grain carefully against her chest, she started down the steeper path.

A pebble slid under her sandal, and she nearly lost her balance. With a sharp little gasp, she caught herself and was able to avoid falling. But her bundle fell from her arms, and with a feeling of guilt at her disobedience, she stopped to pick up the scattered stalks of grain.

It was at that moment that she heard the little sound of pain. Feeling her heart plunge with fear, she stood, hardly breathing, peering down the stony hillside. Had she heard a person or an animal? She remembered Boaz' mention of wolves, and fear touched her coldly. Surely the sound had been human. But — could it be someone deceptively luring a woman with the sound of pain? She almost started to hurry along the path when the sound came again. Could it be a child?

Cautiously she moved away from the path until the valley beside it was visible. There, at the far end, there was a flutter of cloth. Someone or something was lying on the ground.

It's nothing to me, she thought. I'll tell Altah about it, and she can tell Jacob and he can come out to see who or what it is. I'd be foolish to try to go down there, not knowing what I'd find.

The groan came again. Not a woman's voice certainly. All the more reason for her to pass quietly by and go home, Ruth decided.

She started to make her way back toward the path when another movement caught her eye. Stopping, she peered carefully across the gulley to a spot about half way up the opposite hill. There was something there, something as pale as the tan rocks. But it was not a rock. It was an animal crouched almost flat to the ground. Only the fur moving in the first breeze of late afternoon betrayed its presence.

A chill moved across her skin. Boaz had acted as though

he hadn't really believed the story of wolves, but there was no denying the presence of the crouching animal. Perhaps the person who had fallen? — was crouching? — had attracted the wolf's attention so that it had crept out and was now waiting to pounce.

Then surely the person on the valley floor was not trying to set a trap for the passerby. No one, conscious or aware, would lie still so close to a wolf.

But what can I do, Ruth thought in panic. I can't lift a man up this hill. I can't chase a wolf away.

She thought of Boaz and of the new hope for her life, and she was filled with a violent desire to run away from this dangerous situation. There was surely nothing in the world important enough for her to risk her life today of all days.

But almost against her will, her feet were moving out and down until she was finally able to see the person who lay at the bottom of the gulley. The quickening breeze picked up the man's — or was it a boy's? — robe and fluttered it so that for a second she could clearly see the pattern of the cloth. And in that instant, she knew who lay at the bottom of the hill. Only Chalem wore that strip of scarlet sewed to his robe. Aborakim had bought it for him from an Egyptian caravan, the little boy had confided proudly to Ruth, and he carefully attached it to whichever robe he wore. She could remember how clumsily it had been sewed to the cloth, and the memory took her hurtling over the hill. At the same time, the fluttering fur on the other hill blurred as the animal began to slip silently down toward the fallen boy.

"No," Ruth shouted breathlessly. "No!"

She grabbed a rock and flung it across the narrow valley. At least my brother taught Patima and me to throw straight, she thought gratefully. She couldn't tell whether or not the flung stone made the animal stop, but it didn't make any difference. She had to get to Chalem.

In a matter of seconds, she had reached the place where the child lay. It was easy to see what had happened. His

sandal strap was broken and the sandal was twisted sideways on his foot. He had slipped on the treacherous path
and had plunged down the incline, evidently striking his
head on some of the stones as he fell. There was a bloody
gash across his forehead, but he seemed to be breathing
normally, and none of his arms or legs were twisted at that
grotesque angle that indicated a broken bone.

He was only unconscious, then, and it was simply a
matter of picking him up and getting him out of the gulley.
She stooped, grateful for the weeks of stooping in the fields
and slipped her hands under his body. He was heavier than
she anticipated, and she concentrated on getting the proper
leverage.

The sound of a snarl stopped her. She lifted her head
slowly and found herself staring into the face of the wolf.
She saw at once why the animal had dared to come out in
the daylight and why it had risked this human encounter,
why even the stone had failed to deter it. One of its hind
legs had been broken, and the body was gaunt. The wolf
must be crazed with hunger, and the fallen boy had been
too tempting to resist.

Somehow Ruth kept herself quiet although she could feel
a scream of terror building up in her throat. She forced
herself to keep staring into the evil yellow eyes all the while
her hands were sliding further under Chalem, trying to get
a firmer grip on his body, but she was unable to get her
hands far enough under to get a proper hold.

I can't do it, she thought in despair. O Yahweh, help me.
Don't let this child be killed. Send someone, Lord. Send a
man to help me.

Almost at once she felt a curious warmth running
through her body, strengthening her, and slowly she began
to straighten her knees to push herself erect. Something
struck the wolf's side, and it turned clumsily, snarling. In
that second she was standing, hugging Chalem against her
breast.

But the wolf's attention had returned to her, and she was frozen with fear. She heard a sound from the path, and felt, rather than saw, a stone whiz through the air to strike the wolf between the eyes. The stone, Ruth realized, had been flung with the force of a skillfully aimed slingshot. The wolf dropped.

"He may be only stunned," a voice shouted. "Run — run. I'll meet you — "

She was too frightened to obey. Stiffly, numbly, she began to back away from the wolf. She felt a rough hand grab her arm and spin her around. Almost instantly, Chalem was torn out of her arms.

"Run!" Aborakim shouted.

But she could not. Panting, dizzy, sick, she stood swaying, while a rattle of stones behind her indicated that the wolf was beginning to move again.

Aborakim, half way up the hill, turned and saw her still standing where he had left her. He flung Chalem up over his shoulder, so that one hand was free, and raced back to Ruth. Grabbing her roughly, he started to haul her up the hill.

"Hurry," he panted. "Can't you see the animal is crazed?"

She came alive then. She shook Aborakim's hand off her arm and then caught it in her own. She could not tell, as they raced up the hill, whose hand was pulling and whose was clinging.

On the path Aborakim stopped long enough to use his slingshot again, and once more the wolf fell. "If I had only brought my knife," he panted.

"It won't follow," Ruth said. "We only have to worry about Chalem now. My house is closer. We'll take him there."

"All right. Hurry."

When they finally reached the shed, Ruth's strength deserted her, and she sat numbly while Naomi bandaged Chalem's head and bathed his face with water. Aborakim, after he had tumbled his brother into Naomi's lap, stood back watching.

Chalem opened his eyes. "My head hurts," he whimpered while his hand went up to discover the bandage. "What happened?"

"You fell," Ruth said. "You must have been running along the path and slipped on the pebbles."

"I was trying to find Aborakim," Chalem said, "and he always goes along that path. I didn't want him to be angry."

"Why should I be angry?" Aborakim stepped forward.

Chalem's eyes widened. "Because Father is going to marry Ruth. You heard what happened at the city gate."

Aborakim was silent. Naomi looked up, drawing in a quick breath at Chalem's words, but Ruth silenced her with a look.

When Aborakim finally spoke, his voice was stiff. "I'm sure it's none of my business whom Father marries."

Chalem was becoming aware of where he was. "Why are we here? Why did you bring me here, Aborakim?"

"It's natural, isn't it, to take you to the woman who's going to be a sort of grandmother to you?" Aborakim avoided looking at either Ruth or Naomi. "After you had been nearly eaten by a wolf, I needed help from someone."

Chalem's eyes were wide. "A wolf? You're joking."

"I've never been further from joking," Aborakim said. "I'll tell you all about it when you're able to take it in."

Chalem looked wonderingly from one to the other.

"Can you walk?" Aborakim said.

Chalem tested himself gingerly. "Yes. Not easily, perhaps. But I can get home."

"Good. Come then." Aborakim put his arm across his little brother's shoulders. He turned to the women. "Thank you," he said to Naomi. Finally, his eyes met Ruth's. "Thank you for trying to save my brother," he said stiffly.

"Thank you for saving both of us," she answered.

Unexpectedly he flushed like a young child. "It was nothing," he said.

"But to save a Moabite," Ruth began.

Aborakim's eyes dropped but then he looked up. "I didn't even think of you as a Moabite. You were only a woman who had risked her life for my brother."

Ruth felt gratitude filling her. This was the moment for which she had prayed. She smiled at Aborakim, and leaned forward to touch Chalem's shoulder gently. "Now, hurry home," she said, "and the peace of Yahweh be with you both."

"And with you," the boys said like an echo of their father, and turned to go to the house of Boaz.

25

RUTH STOOD alone outside the small shed listening to the sounds of celebration that floated through the air. The whole town of Bethlehem was celebrating the end of harvest. And when darkness had fallen, Boaz and his kinsmen would come to the house of Jacob to claim Ruth as Boaz' wife.

For days the women of Jacob's house, as well as Ruth and Naomi, had been cooking. Now the men were enjoying the feast, and even the women in the back part of the house were tasting the special foods and enjoying a few hours of freedom.

Ruth, whose heart was full to overflowing, had joined in the merriment for a little while, and then had excused herself, saying she had forgotten something in the shed. Now she stood in silence under the fig tree, looking across the town, thinking of all that had happened to her.

Boaz' visit to Naomi had been properly business-like, and not by word or sign had Naomi indicated that she knew Ruth had gone to the threshing floor to ask for Boaz' protection. Ruth was sure now that no one had seen her and no one would ever tarnish her reputation with unsavory gossip. In this, too, Yahweh had granted her everything she had prayed for.

And I a foreigner, Ruth thought with the sense of wonder

which always filled her. Why has He noticed His humblest servant and given her everything the heart could want?

Well, not exactly everything. After that brief interlude when she and Aborakim had shared their strength to save Chalem, Aborakim had retreated again behind a wall of coolness. But if he had thought of her once as a woman — just a woman, not a Moabite — he would again. This was something she simply had to be patient about.

She lifted her head and gazed at the brilliant stars that shone above her. Impulsively, she went to her knees.

"Yahweh, my Lord, my God," she said softly, "I cannot say my feeling of gratitude because I don't know the proper words. You have given me more than I deserve, more than I had ever hoped for. Thank you, Lord, for everything.

"Bless Patima, Lord. She *must* believe in you a little. Make it possible for her to know someday that I'm thinking of her, that I love her, and that I'm going to be the wife of a good man.

"Let me continue to be a good daughter to Naomi. Make me kind and patient even when I don't always feel like it.

"And O Yahweh, my God." Her breath caught. "Let me bear a child. A son. Let me give my lord a son and let him find joy in the child even though it bears Mahlon's name. Oh, please! I won't ask for Aborakim's affection, I won't ask for anything if you will only let me bear a son."

The sound of men's voices came to her, and she got quickly to her feet, aware for the first time that tears were drying across her cheeks. She walked across the yard toward Jacob's house, remembering with what fear and reluctance she had gone to the house of Mahlon when she was fourteen. But now she was a woman and Boaz was kind and good and a godly man. Small wonder that her feet felt winged as she went toward the lighted house. Small wonder that joy filled her until she felt as though she carried the sunrise in her heart.

What if I had stayed in Moab, she thought suddenly. What if I had not believed?

Oh, thank you, Yahweh, she thought again. If I have a son, if Boaz gives me a son, I'll dedicate my life to seeing that he knows about the God of Israel, so that his sons' sons will walk in the way of Yahweh.

So thinking, she pulled her shawl across her face and walked into the house of Jacob, toward the sound of singing and dancing and the cries of "Where is she? Where's the bride?"

Laughing, breathless, she let herself be caught into the merry crowd, let herself be pulled away from the shed that had sheltered her and the woman who had brought her out of Moab, let herself be led to Boaz who stood waiting for her with love in his eyes.

Epilogue

CHALEM BURST INTO THE HOUSE, his face eager. "Ruth," he shouted. "Ruth, where are you?"

"In here. In the big room, spinning. What's wrong?"

"There's a caravan going through Bethlehem. On their way to Moab. I heard one of the drivers speak of Bezer. You can send a message to your sister."

Ruth felt a stab of the same excitement that shone in Chalem's face. She got ponderously to her feet from the stool on which she had been sitting and gazed down at Chalem with delight.

"Is there time to prepare a gift? Will they take it?"

Chalem nodded eagerly. "They're spending the night over near the well. I'll take anything you want me to. You can tell Patima about the baby coming."

Ruth rested her hand on her swollen body with the same sense of awe and wonder that filled her every time she thought of the miracle of the coming child.

"Yes," she agreed happily. "I can tell Patima about the baby."

With Chalem's help, she made up a bundle of small gifts, adding, at the boy's insistence, one of his first clay pots. Even though it was crude, it had a little of the grace and balance that had distinguished Mahlon's work. Patima would see the similarity as surely as Ruth did.

"Be sure to tell the facts clearly," Ruth cautioned when Chalem was ready to take the bundle to the caravan leader. "Tell Patima — everyone in the village will know who she is — that I am married to your father, the finest man in Bethlehem. Tell her that Yahweh has blessed me and that my child is close to birth. Tell her that I'm happy and that I love her very much."

Chalem repeated the message carefully. "Did I say it right?" he asked.

"Put a little more emphasis on the part about Yahweh, our Lord. I want Patima to know He has held me in His hands."

"I'll try," Chalem promised and darted out the door.

It was while she was watching him race down the street that Ruth felt the first real pain. The nagging backache, the mild discomfort of the past several days were suddenly altered into a promise of the imminent birth of her child.

"Mother," she called. "Mother, my time has come."

Naomi was beside Ruth almost before the words were said. "Yahweh be praised!" Naomi exulted. "At last He will give us a child."

It was a long, hard labor, and dawn was edging the world with pearl before Ruth heard the sound she had prayed for — the loud, indignant sound of her child's crying.

"It's a boy," Naomi said in a voice so radiant that no one would ever guess that she was an old woman who had worked all night to help bring the child to birth.

"A son," Ruth exulted. "Will someone wake Chalem and send him to the caravan? I can send word to Patima that — " Her voice broke with exhaustion. "Oh, Mother, let me see him."

"In a minute. When I've cleaned him with salt and oil. Oh, he's beautiful, this boy. With a look of Boaz. How proud Mahlon would be to know that there's a boy to carry on his name."

She came finally to lay the child in the curve of Ruth's

arm. Ruth gazed down at the tiny fingers, the dark lashes fringing the shut eyes, the black hair in damp tufts over the little round head. He was almost ridiculously like Chalem. But, no, the mouth and chin were like Aborakim. It was as though she had had nothing to do with the forming of him at all.

Naomi, who had gone to wake Chalem, came back to the room. "Have you looked enough?" she asked. "There are men outside the room who would like to see the new man in the family."

"Men?" Ruth asked.

"Boaz and Aborakim and Chalem. Chalem refuses to go until he has seen the baby."

"Aborakim?" Ruth's voice wobbled a little because Aborakim's presence was so unexpected.

Naomi smiled. "I told him the baby looked like him and his brother. He had to come to see."

Ruth lay back on her mat and watched Naomi lift the child to carry him to his father.

"A fine boy." Boaz' voice was nearly as wobbly as Ruth's had been. "She has done well. Tell my wife she has given me a fine son."

There was silence then, and Ruth lay in a sort of waiting. Would Aborakim say nothing? Although he was always properly polite to her, there had never been the slightest breaking down of his reserve. He had never once spoken of the birth of the coming child. Certainly there had never been any indication that he planned to acknowledge relationship to the baby when it was born.

Suddenly there was laughter. "Must it be *my* robe?" Aborakim's voice held no irritation, only amusement. "Couldn't you have chosen your other brother for such actions?"

Ruth relaxed. *Your other brother!* Oh, thank you, Yahweh, my Lord and my God. It may be a long time before Aborakim could wholly accept her. But he was accepting her son. It was a beginning!"

"Have you named him?" Altah demanded.

"Not yet." Ruth's seven days of isolation were ended, and she sat smiling around at the neighbors who had crowded in. "Tomorrow when he is circumcised, then he'll be given a name as befits a child of the covenant."

Her eyes met Naomi's and the smile they exchanged was contented. The hours that Naomi had spent teaching Ruth about the laws of Yahweh had been well spent.

"I think Obed would be a fine name," Altah suggested.

Ruth sat thinking about it. "Obed," she mused. "Obed. Servant. Servant of the Most High God. It would be suitable. If my lord agrees, we'll name him that."

Altah's face was shining. "How blessed this house is," she cried. "And how blessed you are," she went on, turning to Naomi. "Ruth has been a wonderful daughter to you — better than seven sons."

Naomi looked at Ruth and then down at the child she held in her arms. "And I once thought I had come back to Bethlehem in bitterness and with empty hands," she confessed. "How wrong I was. Yes, Altah, she is better than seven sons."

Ruth was unable to speak. Turning away, afraid that she would begin to weep, she looked through the door just as Boaz appeared in the opening. Their eyes met and she felt again, as she always did, the rush of joy and love that he created in her.

She remembered the time she had wondered whether or not Boaz reflected his God. Oh, yes, she thought, he was, indeed, a reflection of Yahweh, the God of love and mercy.

And his sons, all of his sons, would be a reflection of him. The goodness of Boaz, his mercy to a foreigner, his generosity to a stranger would be repeated in his sons and his grandsons. And who, in this small town of Bethlehem, could even guess what marvelous shoots would come from the root of Boaz?